A TASTE OF

An island in the Indian Ocean for a wedding present! As if marrying her boss wasn't excitement enough, Cathy thought, as she travelled happily out to Samora to inspect the place. But she arrived to find that the situation was not quite as her fiancé had told her it was, and that there were problems. Notably the unyielding Grant Howard!

Books you will enjoy
by MARGARET MAYO

TORMENTED LOVE

Shangri-La—a deceptively beautiful name for the house Amie had been left in Mauritius, by her unknown uncle. For the house was all he *had* left her; all his money had gone to Oliver Maxwell. It wasn't difficult to conclude that her uncle had hoped she and Oliver would settle the question by marrying each other—but how could she marry a maddening man like that, who didn't care a fig for her anyway?

INNOCENT BRIDE

Jonita couldn't have been in a worse predicament—stranded in Portugal, with no job and not even the fare home. She should have been grateful to Druce Devereux when he came up with a solution to her problem—but she suspected it would only lead her into worse trouble. And how right she was!

PIRATE LOVER

Just about everything had gone wrong with Tammy's holiday in the South of France, and when she lost her handbag and all her luggage into the bargain she reckoned she had reached rock bottom. But no—for next she found herself crossing swords with Hugo Kane, who not only looked like a pirate but behaved like one as well!

BURNING DESIRE

Wild by name and Wild by nature, Leon Wild had been directly responsible for her sister's death, and Janine never wanted to have anything to do with him again. But he had turned up again and it was impossible to avoid him. Impossible, too, to deny that now her love for him was as deep as the hatred she still felt ...

A TASTE OF PARADISE

BY

MARGARET MAYO

MILLS & BOON LIMITED
15-16 BROOK'S MEWS
LONDON W1A 1DR

All the characters in this book have no existence outside the imagination of the Author, and have no relation whatsoever to anyone bearing the same name or names. They are not even distantly inspired by any individual known or unknown to the Author, and all the incidents are pure invention. The text of this publication or any part thereof may not be reproduced or transmitted in any form or by any means, electronic or mechanical, including photocopying, recording, storage in an information retrieval system, or otherwise, without the written permission of the publisher.

This book is sold subject to the condition that it shall not, by way of trade or otherwise, be lent, resold, hired out or otherwise circulated without the prior consent of the publisher in any form of binding or cover other than that in which it is published and without a similar condition including this condition being imposed on the subsequent purchaser.

First published 1981
Australian copyright 1981
Philippine copyright 1981
This edition 1981

© Margaret Mayo 1981

ISBN 0 263 73544 3

Set in Linotype Plantin 11 on 12 pt.

Made and printed in Great Britain by Richard Clay (The Chaucer Press) Ltd, Bungay, Suffolk

CHAPTER ONE

'AN island?' Cathy's blue eyes widened.

Eric nodded and smiled indulgently.

'But it will cost a small fortune!'

'I can afford it,' he replied easily.

She twisted the ring on her finger and gazed at her companion with something approaching awe. 'You would spend all that money on me?'

'For the girl I love cost doesn't enter into it. But I want you to go and see it, give your approval before I finalise the deal.'

'Eric, I love you!' Cathy flung herself into his arms. 'It's the most wonderful present a girl could ever have. You'll come with me, of course?'

He kissed her soundly before holding her at arm's length. 'Afraid not, sweetie.' His clear grey eyes met hers apologetically. 'Not unless you want to forgo the honeymoon?'

'Not on your life!' Cathy tossed her head in pretended anger, her long black hair swinging silkily forward across her face.

With gentle fingers he tucked it behind her ears, cupping her chin in his hands. 'Then you'll have to travel alone—but don't fret, all arrangements have been made. You'll fly out in the morning.'

'So soon?' Cathy was surprised, but because she loved Eric, and because he was offering her the most exciting wedding present a girl could ever have, she did not argue. 'In that case you'd better go so that I can pack.'

But even after he had gone she did not begin immediately. Everything had happened so quickly she could not believe it was true.

Her engagement to Eric Bassett-Brown had been like a dream in the first place. She had worshipped him from a distance ever since joining Bassett Holdings straight from secretarial college, but he had never noticed her. Not until she was promoted to his secretary earlier that year when his father was ill and Eric had been forced to take more interest in the firm. Now his father had died and Eric was in complete control —and she was soon to become his wife!

It still took some getting used to, the thought that in a couple of weeks she would be Mrs Bassett-Brown, with all the prestige that being the wife of the owner of such a company would bring.

She sighed a little and reaching down her case from the top of the wardrobe began to pile into it the few things she thought she would need for a few days on a sunny island. She did wish Eric was going with her, but realised that the pressures of the business would not allow it.

Cathy was up early the next morning ready for what was, to her, the most exciting journey of her life. Eric called for her at eight and drove her to the airport and soon she was on her way.

The first leg of her journey was to the Seychelles, staying overnight, and then a boat to the island of Samora, about a hundred miles south of the Seychelles.

When the plane landed on Mahé Cathy was enchanted. It was a far cry from London's grey streets.

Lush tropical vegetation, coral white beaches, the deep iridescent blue of the Indian Ocean—it was enough to take her breath away.

Her hotel was comfortable and friendly and exotic and she felt a heady anticipation of what was in store. If Samora was anything like this she would not hesitate to accept it as a wedding present. She was beginning to get used to the idea of so expensive a gift and couldn't wait to get there and see for herself exactly what it was like.

Eric had told her nothing, declaring mysteriously that she must make up her own mind and not be influenced by anything he said.

She had never felt so keyed up in her life and when she climbed aboard the boat the next morning her heart was pounding painfully. All she wished was that Eric could be here with her, that they could share her enjoyment, her appreciation of his magnificent offer.

Their journey took them almost two hours, and all the time Cathy was on the lookout for Samora. The cruiser was owned by a friend of Eric's, who informed her that she was very lucky to have 'caught' his bachelor friend.

'I know I am,' she answered, smiling delightfully, her dimples very much in evidence, her dark hair streaming back from her face by the cooling breezes. Her eyes were as blue as the sea and a healthy pink coloured her cheeks.

'Or perhaps I should say that Eric's the lucky one,' said her companion, his eyes lingering appreciatively.

'We both are,' dimpled Cathy graciously. 'How much longer before we reach Samora?'

She was accustomed to flattery, realising modestly that she was an attractive girl with perhaps more than her fair share of good looks. The saying that gentlemen prefer blondes was certainly not true in her case. Her thick, raven-black hair attracted men like bees round honey, but she was used to dealing with them and had no qualms about handling the man at her side should he decide to try and take advantage of their being alone.

But he did no more than look, and a few minutes later he said, 'We're almost there. Any second now the island will come into sight.'

Cathy was on the edge of her toes with excitement, shading her eyes and watching the skyline intently. Samora appeared as a small mound on the horizon, purple and distant, but soon showed its true colours, brilliant green foliage and gleaming white shores, hills and valleys, and an occasional sparkle as the sun reflected on glass.

In less than half an hour she was stepping ashore and saying goodbye to Eric's friend.

'I will pick you up in two days' time,' he said. 'Have fun.'

Eric had certainly been thorough, she thought, as she stood on the powder-soft sand. No detail had been overlooked. She waited until the boat had disappeared before looking about her, thinking with a certain amount of trepidation, 'If I say the word all this can be mine!'

It was not entirely as she had imagined. Her mind's eye had depicted something smaller, the desert island of cartoons, almost. Instead it stretched away as far as the eye could see, green and fertile—and exciting!

The wooden landing stage was new and impressive and a sandy road led away through a miniature forest of palms and takamaka trees. A white house gleamed at the top of a hill, the only indication that the island was inhabited.

As she stood hesitating an ox-drawn cart appeared along the sandy road. The dusky-skinned driver stopped and jumped down, smiling broadly, 'Miss Nielson?'

She nodded and returned his smile.

'Welcome to Samora. I'm from the Hotel Orange. I'm sorry I'm late, but Major's been playing up.'

Major was presumably the ox. He was so tiny that Cathy could not help smiling at his unfortunate choice of name. 'I didn't expect to be met,' she said, 'so don't apologise. I've been admiring your beautiful island.'

He looked pleased and swung her cases easily on to one of the wooden seats, helping her up afterwards and making sure she was settled before coaxing the animal to make the return journey.

Cathy felt that she had been transported back into another age where time stood still. They swept silently along lanes shaded by palms and casuarinas and a peace stole over her that she had never felt in London, and she knew that there was no way that she was going to refuse Eric's offer. This was Utopia!

They drove for almost a mile through the forest before arriving at the Hotel Orange. It was easy to see from where it had got its name. Orange trees surrounded the complex and even grew between the individual chalets themselves, their branches loaded with ripening fruit.

The thought of being able to pick fruit straight from a tree instead of going to the supermarket appealed to Cathy tremendously and she could hardly take her eyes off them. On their journey she had also noticed bananas and other fruits that she could not name. Had anyone ever been so lucky?

The main building was low and sprawling. No wonder she had seen nothing from the shore, she thought. There were no towering hotel blocks here, every building was single-storied, spreading in intriguing shapes into the surrounding vegetation, their roofs thatched, walls snow-white.

It was like nothing she had ever seen before—a taste of Paradise, no less, and it was all going to belong to her!

Inside the hotel she signed the register and was shown to her chalet. Several people nodded and smiled and she felt immediately at ease. There was a serenity here that was missing in London, as though everyone moved around on tiptoe and spoke in hushed voices.

The bungalow was light and airy, cool after the heat of the sun, and more spacious than it had looked from outside. The main room had sliding glass doors so that she could step right outside on to the tiny terrace with its tubs of flaming poinsettias and other tropical flowers.

A bedroom led off from one side, with an adjoining bathroom, and a tiny kitchen from the other—a nice touch, she thought, if anyone felt like cooking for themselves rather than eating in the hotel. It was hardly likely, though, that she would use it herself during her short stay.

Everything was so much to her liking that she wished they were spending their honeymoon here instead of the three-week cruise Eric had planned.

He had made the arrangements himself and she

wondered now why he hadn't thought to combine this trip. It would have been ideal. They could have explored together, made up their minds together.

She suddenly longed for him, and sadness tinged her euphoria. But once she had unpacked and changed into shorts and a halter top, and eaten a delightful lunch in the main dining room, she felt better and was eager to begin her explorations.

Wisely, though, she decided to wait until evening. It was too hot to go walking—instead she took a leisurely swim in the manmade but very natural-looking pool and then rested in the shade on her terrace.

There were scores of people about, but for the moment Cathy preferred to keep herself to herself, daydreaming about the day she would own the island.

She had discovered from the driver of the oxcart that Samora was roughly oval in shape, three miles long and two miles wide, fringed with white sandy beaches, and with a central mountain which was easy to climb from one side but dropped away almost vertically on the other.

Deciding that this hill might be the best point from which to get her first view of the island, Cathy began her climb as soon as some of the heat had gone out of the sun.

Even so perspiration was running freely down her face before she was halfway, and she wished she had thought to bring a drink with her. Perhaps whoever lived at the white house at the top mght offer her some liquid refreshment? She hoped so. No doubt they were used to such requests.

The path zigzagged constantly and Cathy was sure the journey was more like two miles than the half she had been told, but the magnificent views when she finally reached the summit were worth the effort.

From here she could see the whole of the island—the white fringing shoreline, the forests, the vegetation, the sprawling hotel complex and on the other side, more or less immediately below the steep side of the mountain, more bungalows, which she presumed were privately owned.

There were no motor vehicles on Samora, oxcarts were the only means of transport, and she could see several now making their way along the network of sandy roads which criss-crossed the island.

The house, set into the side of the mountain, and which had looked tiny from the shore, was surprisingly large, reached by a flight of steps flanked on either side with a fancy stone balustrade its severe whiteness relieved with dozens of potted exotic looking plants.

The balcony was wide, with white-painted iron furniture and immense red umbrellas, furled at the moment, pointing upwards towards the sky like miniature rockets waiting to take off.

Even though the place looked deserted windows were flung wide, indicating to Cathy that there was someone at home.

She mounted the steps slowly, feeling apprehensive for some unknown reason. She scolded herself savagely. For goodness' sake, all she wanted was a drink. Why be so silly?

Timidly she tapped on the door, and when there was no answer knocked louder. Still no reply. Hesitantly she turned the handle. The door opened to her touch and she saw inside a black and white tiled hall, a gilt chair upholstered in red velvet, and a pyramid of potted plants cascading gracefully in one corner.

'Is anyone there?' she called, quietly at first, but repeating her question loudly when she received no response.

In London she would not have dared enter anyone's house without permission, but here she moved slowly inside. Her mouth was so dry that she must have a drink before she made her way back down. She could not imagine anyone objecting, when they realised they had not heard her arrival.

Each of the rooms she looked into were empty, expensively and beautifully furnished, but unoccupied, and when she found the kitchen Cathy decided to help herself to a glass of water. It was taking a liberty, but there was every chance that the house was empty, even though unlocked, and surely the owner wouldn't begrudge her a drink? She would leave a note, in case they realised someone had been here and wondered who it might be.

She found glasses in a cupboard, stacked haphazardly one on top of the other, but to her horror, as she reached one from the top the whole pile collapsed and shattered on the floor at her feet.

She was so appalled by what she had done that she did not hear footsteps approaching, heard nothing until a rocky voice demanded imperiously, 'What the hell's going on? Who the devil are you, and what do you think you're doing?'

Cathy whirled and was confronted by the hardest, unfriendliest face she had ever seen. She couldn't have spoken had she wanted to. She merely stared, rooted to the spot, wishing the ground would open and swallow her up.

Normally she was not intimidated, could hold her

own with most people, but there was something about this man that would quell even the stoutest of characters.

She felt herself withering beneath his gaze, but for a few moments, no more. Then she asked herself why she was afraid. She had a perfectly legitimate excuse. If he had had the courtesy to answer the door none of this would have happened.

'I'm sorry about the glasses,' she said quickly. 'I'll pay for them, of course. All I wanted was a drink of water. I did knock, but——' She got no further.

'So why didn't you leave?'

The voice was soft, but Cathy was not deceived, and when cold tawny eyes regarded her with belligerent hostility she was the first to look away.

She bent and began to pick up the pieces of glass. 'I was thirsty,' she replied, not looking at him as she spoke. 'It's a long way up the mountain.'

'Then you should have come prepared,' he shot back, 'instead of intruding where you're not wanted.'

His words angered her. 'That's a very unchristian view, Mr—er——?' When he did not answer she continued, 'Are you saying you begrudge me a glass of water?'

'Yes, I do. You're not welcome here, young lady, and I would ask you to leave.'

'Before I've cleaned up this mess?' She spoke sweetly, but her feelings were far from sweet. He disturbed her, this man with the dark tousled hair and harsh antagonistic face.

He was good-looking in a rugged kind of way and there was something vaguely familiar about him that she could not explain. She had certainly never met him before, that much she knew. It would not be easy to forget such a man. Perhaps he reminded her of someone? But she couldn't think who.

His eyes narrowed dangerously. 'I don't find that amusing. Of course you must clean this lot up.'

'And would it be too much to ask if I might take that drink?' Cathy was past caring what he said. She found him unsufferably rude and arrogant, and so far as she was concerned the sooner she left the better.

He nodded—begrudgingly, she thought. 'So long as you don't take too long over it. I have work to do. You're already wasting valuable time.'

Cathy's blue eyes glittered. 'If you expect me to say I'm sorry, I'm not. Have you a dustpan and brush?'

'Somewhere—I expect.' He sounded uninterested. 'You've cut your finger, did you know?'

Cathy didn't. She looked at the spots of blood on the tiled floor, and then at her finger. There was a sliver of glass sticking from it. She gritted her teeth and pulled it out and the blood pumped more quickly than before.

She held it over the sink and looked at her aggressor hopelessly, wondering whether he might offer her a plaster. She hadn't even a hanky to mop up the blood, having left her handbag at the chalet.

'Are you accident-prone?' he asked abruptly, opening a cupboard and taking down a tin box.

'Not usually.' Her reply was indifferent.

'Only when you're in someone else's house?' He turned on the tap and dampened a piece of cotton wool.

Cathy wanted to say that she could manage, that she could attend to the wound herself, but somehow found herself incapable of speech when he took her wrist between strong brown fingers and wiped the cut clean.

He was none too gentle—she hadn't expected him to be—but she didn't protest, holding her breath until he had wrapped a plaster round her finger, letting it go in silent relief when he finished.

He returned the box to the cupboard and resumed his off putting appraisal. Cathy became extremely conscious of her brief white shorts and the green spotted halter top which revealed more than she would have liked this man to see.

Her hair, when she set out, had been tied back, but the ribbon had slipped off ages ago and it now hung in a silken black cascade across her cheeks, her fringe, thick and heavy, hiding her fine brows.

'If it wasn't for the costume,' he said surprisingly, 'I would think it was Cleopatra herself who'd come to visit me.'

It was not the first time Cathy had been paid this same compliment, but she did not feel flattered today. She tossed her head scornfully. 'I certainly don't regard you as Antony! Where did you say that brush was?'

His insolent regard unsettled her. Her heart pounded in a most unusual manner and all she could think of was that the sooner she was away from this inhospitable place the better.

She had felt his aggression when he tended her finger, his anxiousness to be rid of her, a barely controlled irritation—yet he was doing nothing to speed her departure.

He opened a tall cupboard in the corner, revealing an array of brushes and cleaning materials. 'Take your pick,' and he stood back, leaning indolently against the wall, muscular arms folded across a powerful chest, hard eyes still scrutinising.

He wore faded jeans that had certainly seen better days, and a patchy blue singlet that was even more disreputable than his trousers.

From his attitude she had assumed that he was the owner of this house, but looking at him now a sudden doubt entered her mind.

'Exactly who are you?' she demanded. 'What right have you to order me out of this house? If my suspicions are correct you're no more the owner than I am. How do I know you're not an intruder I accidentally disturbed?'

His golden eyes blazed with sudden fury. 'I'm not accustomed to having my identity questioned, young lady, and I'm damn sure I don't have to answer to you!'

He jerked a broom out of the cupboard and thrust it at her so violently that she stumbled backwards, only saving herself by grasping the cupboard door. It shuddered beneath her weight and the hose from the cleaner fell with a clatter to the floor.

The big man swore violently and without another word left the room. Cathy picked up a tin of polish and flung it after him. Curse the man, it was all his doing!

What she had not counted on was the fact that he might have second thoughts. He reopened the door a split second before the polish reached it, receiving its impact full in his face.

Cathy clapped her hands to her mouth, staring in fascinated horror. She didn't know whether to laugh or cry, but when she saw that he was not hurt, that the tin had bounced off him as it would have the door itself, she began to giggle, and the more angry he became the funnier she thought it was.

She did not stop until he strode across the room and

took her by the shoulders, shaking her so violently that her teeth rattled.

'I'm s-sorry,' she gasped. 'I didn't expect you to c-come back.' Her wide blue eyes looked up at him with unconscious appeal.

'You deserve punishment,' he rasped savagely. 'Not content with wrecking my home you even try to hurt me. Get the hell out of here before I do something I'll regret!' He thrust her from him and turned his back.

In those few seconds while his hands had rested on her shoulders Cathy had been aware of his immense strength, of a dynamic physical attraction, and instead of running she stood there hesitantly, staring at his broad back, tempted to try and offer another apology.

For a few moments all was silent, then slowly he pivoted to face her. His tawny eyes, flecked with gold she noticed at close range, were enigmatic, resting coolly upon her face.

She felt hypnotised, could not have moved had she wanted to. She wondered what he would do next, felt a curious urge to find out whether he was immune to her. Most men weren't, especially if they found themselves alone with her.

Unconsciously her lips parted and she moistened them with the tip of her tongue, her pulse rate increasing dramatically.

His eyes narrowed and he took a step towards her. She realised suddenly that he had thought she was inviting his advances, and just as abruptly she remembered Eric!

But it was too late. Tremendously powerful arms pulled her roughly against the muscular hardness of him, full cool lips closed on hers in a brutally punishing kiss that sent her reeling, one broad capable hand slipped inside her brief top cupping her breast.

She struggled angrily for a few seconds. This wasn't what she had wanted. How dared he try to take advantage!

But beneath the urgent pressure of his mouth her lips parted, her breathing became ragged, her throat ached, and unable to help herself she responded to his kisses. All thoughts of Eric fled and time stood still.

With unexpected exasperation he thrust her from him. 'Just as I expected,' he rasped harshly. 'You came here for one reason only—I should have known! You're not the first girl who's tried to force her attentions upon me. Is it money you're after, or the publicity when you spread the news that you've been to bed with me?'

Cathy was enraged. Her ecstasy disappeared to be replaced by burning anger. 'My God, you fancy yourself. Bed—with you? It's the last thing I'd ever do!' She held out her hand with its brilliant solitaire diamond. 'I already have a man, thank you, and I'm more than satisfied.'

He looked at her disbelievingly. 'The poor blighter has my sympathies. But if it wasn't my body you were after what exactly did you want?'

'I told you,' she replied distinctly. 'A drink of water, though I've lost all hope of ever getting that.'

'Oh, you can have one,' he returned smoothly. 'I'll get it myself.'

She watched incredulously as he filled a glass at the sink, had almost convinced herself that he had had a change of heart, when unexpectedly she received the contents full in her face.

'Touché,' he said in a satisfied sort of voice, ignoring

her anger and regarding her with a cool contemplation that irritated her beyond endurance. 'Clean the mess up and then go, will you?'

Her chin jerked. 'And if I refuse?'

'It wouldn't be wise,' he said, eyes narrowed.

She looked at him in mock disbelief. 'What would you do?'

'Try me and find out,' was all the satisfaction she got.

She decided not to risk it, instead getting down on her knees and sweeping up the fragments of glass, emptying the pan into a pedal bin in the corner. She checked to make sure there were no pieces left and then looked across to where he stood by the door.

He had watched her every move and she could feel high colour in her cheeks, and she was more thirsty than ever before. 'I think that's it,' she said, striving to keep her voice steady. 'If you'd just let me out, I'll give my word that I won't disturb you again.'

His smile was sardonic. 'You expect me to believe that? But since my work has now been well and truly interrupted why don't you stay for that drink you—er —claimed was all you were after? I've a notion to hear something about yourself.'

Cathy regarded him suspiciously, was tempted to fling his offer in his face, but her thirst won. It was a long way back and she would feel better able to make the journey if she was refreshed. Reluctantly she nodded.

He opened the door. 'We'll sit on the terrace, it's pleasant there. You know your way? I'll be out in a few minutes.'

Cathy retraced her steps outside and sat down on one of the white iron chairs, pondering on the turn of events. To say they had taken her by surprise would be an understatement. She had never dreamt of the possibility of meeting someone like *him*. He was unlike anyone she had ever known, and she both hated and begrudgingly admired him. He had that air of power combined with raw masculinity that so few men have. Even Eric with his millions and his thriving business could not meet up to this unknown man.

Who was he? she wondered, again puzzled by his vague familiarity. A celebrity, perhaps? Someone she had seen on television? Could be he was a sportsman or an athlete. He had an athlete's build; powerful, dynamic, muscular.

In her mind's eye she could see again that dark curly hair and striking chiselled features, his disreputable clothes and those square tanned hands. She trembled at the thought of them touching her skin and her own hand involuntarily touched her breast where his had been.

An unfamiliar ache settled in her stomach and she closed her eyes, asking herself what was the matter. Why should she feel emotionally disturbed due to meeting this unfriendly stranger? She was engaged to Eric, wasn't she? She had no right allowing herself to even think this way about another man.

She tried telling herself that this was a chance meeting, that their paths would not cross again. But if Eric bought the island, what then? It was too much to suppose that they would not meet.

The chink of glasses brought her out of her reverie and she looked up at her host as he settled the tray on to the table in front of her.

He wore sunglasses, hiding completely his expressive eyes. She supposed she ought to be grateful she could not see his undoubted hostility, could pretend that they were friends, but she wasn't.

It was as though he was hiding himself behind a mask and she felt curiously uneasy, inquisitive even.

He unfurled the umbrella over their table and sat down. She was distinctly aware of his presence and hoped it did not show.

'Shall I pour the drinks?' she asked in a small voice that sounded nothing like her own, but irritated her in case he guessed the unnerving effect he had.

He nodded and settled back in his seat, watching as she filled the bottom of each glass with crushed ice before pouring in the delicious-looking lime. Cathy handed his to him and was convinced it was not accidental when his fingers touched hers for a shock-filled second.

What's the matter with me? she asked herself irritably. Why do I let this man disturb me when I have a loving fiancé waiting at home? She could not answer and picked up her own glass with fingers that were not quite steady. She took a long cooling drink, unaware that he was observing her closely.

'You certainly needed that. Perhaps I should apologise for having kept you waiting so long?'

Cathy said sharply, 'It would certainly give me pleasure to hear you say you were sorry, but I know for a fact that you wouldn't.'

His lips quirked humorously. 'How do you know?'

'Because you don't strike me as a man who would say he was sorry to anyone.'

His thick brows rose above the glasses, lines furrowing his broad forehead. 'Go on, then, tell me what sort of a man you think I am. I should be interested to hear.'

'You might not like it.'

'I've had many things said to me in the past that I haven't liked,' he said, 'but I've broad enough shoulders to take it, so go ahead, give me your verdict.'

He was goading her now, she knew, and she wished she hadn't attempted to get the better of him in the first place. No one would ever do that.

But she shrugged and said confidently, 'Very well, you asked for it. In my opinion you're a person to be avoided at all costs. As a matter of fact I'm still not entirely sure that you own this house. You could be a squatter—your clothes don't entirely add up with the rest of the place.'

She paused, wondering what sort of reaction she was getting, but all he did was sit there watching her from behind his dark glasses.

'On top of that, I would say that you have a very high opinion of yourself, you like to be in command of every situation, you're aggressive, rude, uncaring about other people's feelings—is that enough, or shall I go on?' How she wished she could read his expression!

'It's enough for starters. Would you like to hear what I think about you?'

Cathy had not expected this and her blue eyes widened. 'Not really, but I expect you'll tell me all the same.'

In the distance was the murmur of the sea and the faint rustling of leaves disturbed by an early evening breeze. The sun was pleasantly warm and it could have all been so perfect had she been here with Eric instead of this off putting stranger whose identity she did not even know.

'First of all,' he said abruptly, 'you're engaged to a man you don't love.'

Cathy glared, surprised into sudden anger. 'That's a lie! I'm very much in love with my fiancé. How dare you insinuate such a thing!'

'Then how do you account for your reaction to my kiss?' he asked smoothly. 'If you love this man as much as you say, you'd be immune to all others.'

He waited a moment before continuing, 'Secondly, you're out for a good time—otherwise you would never have entertained the idea of coming without your good man.'

'How do you know he's not on Samora with me?' countered Cathy hotly, highly indignant at the accusations he was making.

'Because you would be together, like all young lovers.'

'Huh!' she exclaimed derisively.

'And finally, you're not going to get what you want from me.'

'Oh, don't say we're back to that again,' cried Cathy. She finished her lime juice and stood up. 'If your only intention is to insult me then I'm going. Thanks for the drink, and goodbye!'

He caught her wrist in a crushing grip and yanked her back down. 'No one walks out on me in the middle of a conversation. I've not finished with you yet, young lady.'

Cathy stared stubbornly in front of her, aware of an excruciating pain in her wrist but unwilling to give him the satisfaction of knowing he had hurt.

A few long seconds passed before he spoke again. 'Okay, so why are you on Samora? A last-minute fling before you hook some poor fellow for life? Or had you already decided that he was not the one for you and wanted to get away from it all to make up your mind?'

'Neither,' said Cathy distantly. 'As a matter of fact, if you must know, I've come to have a look at the island. Eric's going to buy it for me as a wedding present.'

She had hoped to impress him, was prepared for any reaction other than the one she got.

'Eric?' He snatched off his glasses. 'Not Eric Bassett-Brown, by any chance?' The tanned face was harsh, his eyes cruelly intent.

Cathy's well shaped brows rose. 'You know him?'

He nodded. 'A devious move. Send in the fair sex, was that what he suggested? It's not on. Tell him that, will you? He's wasting his time—and money.'

She was perplexed, and showed it, frowning furiously. 'Do you mind telling me what you're talking about!'

'Don't come the innocent with me, miss,' he rasped. 'I know what his little game is. He was taking a chance, though, sending you, or doesn't he care what happens to you so long as he can get his hands on Samora?'

His face was creased into an ugly scowl, jawline taut, hands clenched, resting on the table in front of him. There was power in those fists and Cathy felt afraid. She wished he would explain so that she might understand. He had clearly got the wrong impression as to why she was here.

'What do you know about Eric wanting to buy Samora?' she asked anxiously.

Thick bushy brows rose scornfully. 'That he's been trying to persuade me to sell for years. I don't much care for his new tactics either—no disrespect to yourself, of course.'

'*You*—own Samora?' She had had no idea. She was shattered. It was the last thing she had expected.

CHAPTER TWO

'You act well,' said the big man. 'Eric was right to put his faith in you. A pity he underestimated me, though. It would have saved you this unnecessary journey.'

'I'm not acting,' returned Cathy hotly. 'I came here at Eric's suggestion, yes, but only because he said he wanted to buy it for me for a wedding present.'

'And the moment the deal went through, *if* it had gone through, he would have dropped you like a red-hot brick. He's using you, pretty lady, in case you didn't know. How long have you known him?'

'Years,' lied Cathy airily.

He looked at her closely. 'I don't believe you. Eric had a different girl last year. I know, because he brought her here.'

He sounded so confident that Cathy began to feel doubts creep in, but she kept them to herself. 'So what, we weren't engaged then.'

'Come on, you weren't even going out with him.' Tawny eyes flashed in her direction, disbelieving, antagonistic.

Cathy shrugged. 'I still knew him. I've worked for his company ever since I left college.'

His eyes lightened. 'Ah, I see it all now. He took a choice of the women at his disposal. Flattered, were you, when he singled you out for preferential treatment?'

It was exactly what had happened, but Cathy was

sure it couldn't be for the reasons this man was suggesting. Yet in one way it made sense. She had been surprised when Eric suggested she make this trip alone, had thought it rather strange, but had seen no ulterior motive behind his request.

'I think you're mistaken,' she said spiritedly. 'If Eric had wanted me to—to get round you—well, he would have told me, but he made no mention of you. I hadn't a clue who this island belonged to. So far as I knew it was up for sale, otherwise how would he have known about it?'

He shook his head as if unable to follow her reasoning. 'Eric wants it, and what Eric wants he usually gets. He's of the opinion that money can buy anything, haven't you found that out? I'm surprised if you haven't. It's how he gets most of his girls.'

He had certainly been lavish with his money, Cathy had to admit, but she had never for one moment suspected him of trying to *buy* her. She would have loved him whether he was rich or poor.

'Money has made no difference to our relationship,' she returned hostilely. 'Eric loves me and I love him, and that's all there is to it. You've no right to suggest anything so despicable! I shall tell Eric when I get back, he'll make you apologise.'

He laughed mirthlessly. 'Tell me another funny story. Eric is far more devious than you give him credit for. He knew exactly what he was doing when he sent you here.' His eyes flicked her body insolently. 'You see, he knows the type of woman I like. He couldn't have chosen anyone better. He decided, in his own warped mind, that I would fall for you, that before long I would be your passive slave, willing to do anything you ask. My God, he was mistaken!'

'You mean I'm not your type?' Cathy didn't know why she asked that, why she felt hurt.

He looked her up and down slowly. 'Oh yes, you're my type all right, he's done his homework on that point. What he seems to have overlooked is that my desire to hang on to Samora is stronger than my desire for another woman. Living alone suits me, I have no wish to alter my life style.'

'And you can afford to turn down Eric's offer?' Cathy looked askance at his shabby clothes.

'Don't be deceived,' he said softly, almost menacingly. 'I dress this way because I prefer it. Samora is my retreat, where I can be myself and not give a damn what anyone thinks.'

'I don't suppose you would anyway,' muttered Cathy. Without waiting to be invited she refilled her glass. All this talking had made her thirsty again. 'I can't quite see where this conversation has got us,' she remarked primly after taking a long satisfying swallow, 'but I see no point in remaining any longer. Am I allowed to go now?'

A hint of a smile lifted the corners of his mouth, his earlier anger had disappeared. 'If you like, or you could stay and have dinner.'

Cathy said quickly, suspiciously, 'I thought I was holding you up from your work, whatever that might be, Mr—er——?'

'Howard. Grant Howard. And no, I shall not work again today. Let's say my thoughts have been disrupted far too much—Cleopatra.' There was a quirk of one eyebrow as he said the name, and something suggestive lurked behind his golden eyes, putting Cathy instantly on her guard.

She ought to refuse, she knew, but the offer was

tempting. If she went back to her chalet it would be for a lonely meal. At least here the company was stimulating, if nothing else.

'Then I'll accept, if you don't object to my inappropriate dress—and my name's Cathy.'

'As I myself don't give a damn what I wear,' he said, smiling, satisfied, 'it matters little to me whether you're wearing an expensive evening gown or—nothing, and I think I prefer Cleopatra, Cathy. It suits you. Cathy suggests someone sweet and innocent, not the sultry seductress I see before me.'

'I'm no such thing!' Cathy's blue eyes flashed heatedly. 'You misinterpret me, if that's what you think.'

'I do?' Eyebrows rose disbelievingly, golden eyes held hers so that once again she was the first to look away. 'If you don't mind me leaving you,' he said at length, 'I'll go and see about dinner. It's only a cold meal, I'm afraid. My housekeeper has left it all ready.'

Cathy looked at him. 'Do you want any help?' she asked reluctantly.

His lips quirked. 'I thought you'd never ask.'

She could have hit him. 'Don't be insulting, Mr Howard, or I might change my mind about staying.'

'And you think that would bother me?'

'No,' she admitted slowly, only too well aware he had suggested she stay out of politeness, or perhaps curiosity. She dimpled sweetly. 'I have the impression that you shut yourself away here to get away from women.'

'To get away from all mankind,' he amended testily.

'Why? Do you hate the human race so much?'

He shook his head. 'You misconceive me.' He stood over her, a towering man, broad and powerful, smiling sensuously, and Cathy felt a physical awareness tingling through her limbs.

Whoever he was, whatever he was, he had an immense magnetism, a virility that must surely be felt by all who came into contact with him, and she was convinced that he was deliberately setting out to attract her now, no doubt to prove himself right when he had said she was attempting to seduce him. He would be expert at twisting any situation to his advantage, she was sure.

'I don't live here all the time,' he continued. 'But for the periods I do, peace and quiet is my aim.'

'And where do you live for the rest of the year?' she asked politely, feeling that this was expected of her —not that she wanted to know, she told herself. What he did was his affair, she couldn't care less.

'Many things. I travel a great deal, do a bit of this and that—but I'm sure you're not really interested. Or is it all part of the plan to win me over?'

Cathy tossed her head scornfully, her black hair swinging across her face. She looked at him from beneath its protective shield. 'You too misconceive me, Mr Howard. Shall we drop the subject?'

He bent down and took her chin between firm brown fingers, planting an unexpected kiss firmly on her lips. 'A good idea.' He took her hand and pulled her up. 'Let's go and see about dinner.'

She was trembling and hated herself for it. She was engaged to Eric and she must remember that. This reaction she felt, it was nothing more than antagonism, revulsion. It had to be. There was no way that she could like Grant Howard.

They ate their meal on the terrace—avocado filled with a mouthwatering concoction of prawns in a creamy sauce, followed by salad with a whole baby chicken, washed down with plenty of white wine, and a basket of fresh fruit from which to take her pick.

She felt deliciously replete afterwards. Grant Howard had surprisingly set himself out to be charming company, all his earlier antagonism gone. He was widely knowledgeable about many subjects and it had been a long time since she had spent such a pleasant evening.

Afterwards, when they had carried their plates back into the kitchen, Cathy suggested he allow her to wash up.

'Leave them,' he said peremptorily. 'My housekeeper will see to it in the morning.'

'But I'd like to,' she insisted, 'it's the least I can do after you've so generously shared your meal with me.'

'Payment for your supper?' he mocked. 'I can think of better ways.'

'I've no doubt you can,' she returned, 'but if you don't mind, I'll choose this one.'

He seemed amused. 'Suit yourself, but don't expect me to help. A tea towel in my hand is not the image I see of myself.'

Nor could she. Besides, those big hands would undoubtedly be clumsy handling the delicate china. 'I wouldn't dream of asking you. Kindly leave me alone, Mr Howard, and I'll have this lot done in next to no time.'

It was a relief to be alone, away from the stifling atmosphere of his presence. When he was in the room she was conscious of nothing else, even all thoughts of Eric fled, and she felt guilty. She was being disloyal, but she couldn't stop herself, and the doubts Grant had planted in her mind were growing alarmingly.

Little things to which she had previously attached no significance now reared their heads. Eric's sudden interest in her, their brief courtship. The fact that he had done the booking for this trip, and their honeymoon, himself. Why hadn't he asked her to fix them up? She was his secretary, all other trips she had arranged for him, so why not these?

In view of what Grant had said she wondered whether Eric had in fact booked their honeymoon— or would their engagement be over once she got back, once she had supposedly got on the right side of the indomitable Grant Howard?

Eric must have known exactly what would happen, that Grant would tell her he had previously refused to sell the island, and relied on her startling good looks to clinch the deal where he himself had failed.

In all fairness to Eric, she would wait until she returned to England to hear his side of the story, but it was disturbing all the same.

She did not like to feel that she was being used, that her love for him was one-sided, and she hoped she would find it all a mistake. Nevertheless she felt very bitter when she left the kitchen in search of Grant Howard.

She had assumed he would return to the terrace, but it was empty and she felt lost. Should she leave now, or seek him out in the house? What did he expect? Would he be angry if she took up more of his time?

She was standing dithering when he appeared. He smiled warmly, heartstoppingly. 'We may as well make a night of it, Cleopatra. I have music playing inside, come and join me.'

What had happened to his insistence that he liked to be alone? she wondered, but she was unable to refuse. He had some sort of power over her that she could not understand, and at this moment, while she was feeling so depressed about Eric, she did not particularly want to try and fathom it out.

He took her to a long airy room at the back of the house. It was carpeted in green and one whole wall was filled with sliding glass doors which were open, revealing breathtaking views of immaculately kept gardens, tiering up the hill towards the summit. Plants overflowed into the room itself and it was like an extension of outside. Cathy immediately thought of it as the garden room.

Soft, sweet music came from one corner where there was all kinds of expensive audio equipment. One half of the room was clear of furniture, perfect for dancing, and the remainder held deep armchairs covered in jungle print.

It was a restful room where one would find it easy to relax, but somehow Grant Howard did not strike her as a restful person. She could imagine him pacing the room like a caged tiger, changing one record for another, never still for one moment.

His physique suggested an active life and she guessed that he thrived on it—why then had he told her that he came here for peace and quiet? But he had also said that he worked here! What type of work could he do in this sleepy place? He intrigued her, there was no doubt about that.

She sat down in one of the chairs that seemed to eat her up, eyeing him as he dropped across another, legs hanging loosely over the arm.

Neither spoke for a long time. He studied her intently and despite the fact that his scrutiny made her grow warm she managed to return his gaze, and the more she looked at him the more she liked what she saw, which was ridiculous after the way he had treated her in the beginning.

Amazingly he struck her as a totally honest man. She could not imagine that he would lie about Eric, he had no reason to, and she felt a growing unhappiness that the man she had become engaged to had apparently treated her so shabbily.

'How did you meet Eric?' she asked abruptly.

He did not seem surprised by her question. 'We were at Oxford together. Since then we've met infrequently—the more infrequent the better so far as I'm concerned. Eric uses people too much for my liking!'

'He's not using me,' Cathy declared positively.

'Guilty conscience?' he mocked. 'In point of fact I wasn't thinking about you, but he is, since you mention it, whether you like it or not—and I think you're beginning to realise it.'

Cathy's blue eyes sparked. 'You like to think you know a lot about me, Mr Howard. What makes you so sure?'

'I study people. It's part of my job.'

'And what is your job?' she asked pertinently.

He smiled mysteriously. 'I'm surprised you don't know. I'm usually recognised on sight.'

'Did it pique you that I didn't?' Though there had been that hint of familiarity! She must have seen his picture somewhere; on the television, or in the papers, perhaps? She frowned, trying to recollect where it had been.

'Not in the slightest. It's a refreshing change to meet

someone who doesn't know me, or know of me. It saves the usual barrage of questions.'

'To which you object?'

'Not always, but it can be irritating.' The record finished and he rose to turn it over.

Cathy noticed that he had neatly avoided answering her question, which made her all the more intrigued, and almost without realising it her eyes followed him across the room, mentally assessing, admiring even. He was a forceful character, not a sort she had come across before. Even Eric, with all his money, was weak compared to this man, and though she hated to admit it, she found herself becoming more and more attracted by the minute.

It was time to go, she told herself, before she did something silly. He had set the scene—a perfect meal, sufficient wine to make her feel heady without being drunk, and now this beautiful peaceful room and the soft sensuous music.

It occurred to her that he could be attempting a seduction scene, precisely what he had accused her of earlier, and her heartbeats quickened. He was an exciting, stimulating, fullblooded male animal who could set any woman's pulses racing.

She stood up, and he turned, frowning.

'I'm going,' she said quietly. 'I—I don't want to outstay my welcome. I know you have work to do, so I will let you get on with it.'

He came across and took her hands in his. 'Afraid, Cleopatra? Think you've bitten off more than you can chew?'

She was immediately aware of his sexual virility, there was an almost tangible aura emanating from him, and she knew even before she made her protest that she had lost. 'Nothing of the kind, Mr Howard. I think it's time I went, that's all. Thank you for an excellent meal.'

She tugged her hands, but to no avail—and he wasn't even trying! His strength was far superior to hers.

'Try calling me Grant,' he said softly. 'And the night is young, what's your hurry?'

'I happen to be engaged to another man, *Mr* Howard, that's what.'

'So,' he shrugged, 'have I made any improper advances? Anything to which you think Eric might object?' Without waiting for her to answer he continued, 'It's all in your mind, sweet seductress. If you want it to happen it will, and you know it. Stay and prove to me that you're not what I first thought.'

The challenge could not be ignored. Cathy stared at him defiantly. 'Very well—Grant. What would you suggest we do next?'

His liquid eyes challenged her. 'The choice shall be yours, sweet lady. We can sit and talk, drink a little, dance a little, whatever you wish.'

'I'd like a drink,' she said suddenly. The contact between them was electric. Did he feel it too? Was he deliberately touching her?

'Whatever Cleopatra wishes.'

The instant he released her she felt bereft, and angry—angry with herself for entertaining such emotions when it was Eric she loved. These feelings for Grant—what were they? Pure animal reaction? It had to be—he was an exciting, presentable male, despite the shabby clothes; any woman would be attracted.

He handed her a glass of amber-coloured liquid that matched his eyes. 'To a pleasant evening.'

There was mockery in his voice and Cathy said sharply, 'But one begrudgingly given?'

An eyebrow rose. 'I wouldn't say that. No one but a fool would turn away a temptress like you.'

Cathy had been called some things in her life, but never a temptress or a seductress, and she did not like it. She felt insulted, degraded, and her eyes flashed hostilely. 'Grant Howard, my motives for coming here were quite genuine. I don't like what you're insinuating.'

'You're not flattered?'

'Far from it. If you think I'm of easy virtue you're mistaken. Don't think I can't see through you. I know what the soft music and fine words are leading up to.'

'Then you know more than me. Are you expecting me to make a pass? Perhaps even looking forward to it?' His fingers lightly touched her bare shoulders, moving expertly beneath her heavy hair, sending shivers of delight through her body.

She was paralysed, wanting him to carry on, yet knowing that she ought to stop him. Eric had never affected her like this, but come to think of it, Eric had never been very romantic. He had showered her with presents, openly declared his love, but that was all. There had been no intimacies between them, he had never touched her like this man now, never made her feel quite so deliciously feminine and desirable.

Her bare legs brushed against the rough denim of his jeans, felt the power in those muscular thighs. His head lowered and his lips traced the column of her throat. 'Why don't you stop me?' he whispered.

Cathy tried to speak but couldn't. Her throat ached with quelled passion and she closed her eyes so that she shouldn't see him. She felt her drink taken from her, his arms wrapped firmly about her waist, her body pressed tightly against his, his own vibrant response to her slim compliant form.

It was a new and exhilarating feeling and even though she knew he was doing it deliberately, that his feelings for her were non-existent and he was merely making the most of the situation, she still could not bring herself to push him away.

She felt drugged, lightheaded, and had absolutely no control over herself. He knew what he was doing, this man. He was no fool when it came to women, that was clear.

'You're disappointing me, Cleopatra. You're proving me right.'

The goading words were the incentive she needed. Her beautiful eyes shot wide and she struggled to free herself, his triumphant laugh and the victory on his face inciting her anger, so that as soon as he released her she lashed out.

Inevitably she missed because his reaction was quicker than hers. He wagged a finger admonishingly. 'Temper, temper, my passionate friend. You must learn to control it.'

'With you around that's impossible,' she snapped. 'You're the most loathsome man I've ever met!'

'Yet you almost allowed me to make love to you. I wonder why?'

'Oh, go to hell!'

He picked up her glass and put it back into her hand. 'Drink up, pretty lady. The situation is of your own making.'

'I like that!' she blazed. 'All I came here for was a drink of water, not to get raped!'

He frowned strongly, angrily. 'You're in no danger of that. My code of ethics wouldn't allow it.'

'You surprise me.' Her eyes were wide with disbelief. 'Don't men like you grasp at anything within their reach?'

'And what's that supposed to mean?' he asked harshly, eyes darkening.

She had clearly angered him further, and the trouble was she didn't know herself what she meant. She had spoken without thinking. 'If you don't know I'm not going to enlighten you,' she continued brightly, 'and I really do think it's time I went now. May I use your bathroom?'

He inclined his head graciously, though there was still a flintlike expression on his handsome face. 'Second on the left along the corridor.'

Cool green marble greeted her, screaming opulence. Everything about the place spelt wealth—all except the man himself. Either his money meant nothing to him—or he was still lying and the house did not belong to him.

She did not care any more, all she wanted was to get out, return to her little chalet where she could be alone, with no hulk of a man disturbing her as had no other person in her whole life.

He was nowhere in sight when she emerged and she did not bother to try and find him. She left the house quickly and almost ran down the hillside, without once looking back.

She was breathless by the time she reached her bungalow and the first thing she did was turn on the shower in an attempt to wash away any lingering impression of Grant Howard's hands on her body.

She did not succeed. An hour later as she lay in bed she could still feel the warm hardness of him against her, the pressure of his lips, and she knew that when she slept she would dream of him.

He had made a distinct impression and it would be a long time before she forgot him. All she could hope was that their paths would not cross again before she left Samora.

Another two days! How she wished she had had the presence of mind to ask the boatman where he could be contacted. She had never envisaged anything like this happening, had no idea that she might want to leave before the end of her allotted time.

It had all seemed so idyllic in the beginning, would be still, so long as Grant Howard kept out of her way, or she his. Perhaps, she thought hopefully, he never left his house, in which case there would be no problem. She certainly had no intention of going up there again—ever.

She soon fell asleep, the events of the day taking their toll, and surprisingly she did not dream. She slept deeply and peacefully and woke the next morning completely refreshed, able to laugh at her fears of the night before.

She spent a few hours after breakfast lazing outside her bungalow, occasionally swimming, not once looking up at the hill which dominated Samora, with its white house on the top occupied by that lethal combination of arrogant good looks and magnetic sex appeal.

It was difficult to get him out of her mind, but she was determined, and after a solitary lunch in the hotel Cathy picked up a book left by one of the former occupants of the chalet, sitting in the shade on her tiny terrace.

It was not her type of book, although she knew it was an international best-seller, as were all Howard Grant's books. He was virtually a household name, renowned as much for the way he researched his books as for his writing.

It was not until she saw the photograph on the back cover that Cathy realised exactly who he was. She should have recognised him immediately, his face had been in the papers enough times; even his name, Grant Howard, should have told her. Yet that simple inversion had done the trick. She had had no idea—just a vague awareness of having seen his face somewhere before.

No wonder he had been cross when she disturbed him! He must do his writing here. Presumably everyone else on the island knew, had been warned to keep away from the white house.

She couldn't help it, though, could she? She hadn't known, no one had thought fit to tell her—and it was what Eric had planned! Her thoughts halted abruptly. She was being disloyal. She must wait for Eric's own story before condemning him.

For a long time she studied the photograph. His wild curly hair was tamed here, he wore a collar and tie, but the expression in those light eyes might have been for her. He looked as though he had recently made love. They were alive, vibrant, and tormented her as they looked out from the page.

'Now you know.'

She did not have to look up to discover to whom the deep throaty voice belonged. 'Why didn't you tell me?' she asked at length.

'It suited me not to. Mind if I join you?'

'Yes, I do,' she snapped irritably. 'Like you yesterday, I fancy solitude at this precise moment.'

'Why?'

It was a reasonable question but one to which she had no answer. Merely looking at his photograph had disturbed her, but to have him here as well, to feel the full force of his physical attraction, was something she did not want, something she had been trying to fight against ever since last night.

'No particular reason,' she said defensively. 'I feel like reading, that's all.'

'Are you a fan of mine?'

She looked up at him from beneath her long lashes. 'Sorry to say, no.'

'Then why my book?'

'Because it's the only one available. I found it in the chalet.'

His lips twisted wryly. 'A few more like you and I'll be on the breadline!'

'I doubt it,' she said quickly. 'Your books sell by the million, that much I know.'

'What else do you know about me?' Despite her insistence that she wanted to be alone he sat down on the floor, leaning back against the wall of the chalet.

'I've read your reviews,' she admitted. 'Another best-seller from the mighty pen of red-hot author Howard Grant. Is that your real name, or the version you gave me?'

'Grant Howard. It's surprising how many people don't instantly realise the connection.'

'It must afford you a great deal of amusement.'

'Relief, actually. It's no fun being in the limelight all the time.'

Cathy put down the book, resigning herself that she was not to read this afternoon. 'Do the islanders know who you are?'

He nodded. 'Most of them—and they respect my privacy.'

'A dig at me? I didn't know.'

'I'm beginning to believe you,' he said surprisingly. 'What I can't understand is why you allowed yourself to get caught by Bassett-Brown.'

'I love him,' she said simply.

'Rubbish! I suspect you were in love with the idea of being in love, especially to some rich business tycoon. It can turn a girl's head. I know, I've had my fair share of the experience.'

'Lucky you,' she returned drily. 'Why are you here now? Why aren't you writing?'

He studied her intently. 'Because a certain young person resembling Cleopatra has disturbed my thoughts.'

Cathy didn't believe him. He had disturbed hers, she freely admitted that, but as for her distracting him, it was ludicrous. 'Am I expected to believe that?'

'Not unless you want to,' he shrugged.

'Then I shan't. Can I offer you a drink?'

'A cup of tea would be nice. No one out here seems able to make it exactly the same as the English.'

He followed her into the kitchen and his presence dominated the room so that Cathy could not think straight and wished he had remained outside. When eventually the tea was made he took the tray from her, carrying it out on to the terrace.

She found another chair and they sat side by side listening to the sounds of the ocean. She forced herself to think about Eric, determined not to accept that he might have tricked her. Perhaps Grant did not like Eric very much and had said this to break up their engagement? It was a problem that she was undecided how to solve. She wanted to believe Grant, but she did not like the thought that Eric could have made a fool of her.

Soon, in the dominating presence of Grant Howard, all thoughts of her fiancé faded and she began to wonder why this man had sought her out when he had made no bones yesterday about telling her that he required privacy. Why exactly had he come down here today? She did not feel flattered. She felt an anger mingling with her growing awareness. What game was he playing? Why was he doing this to her?

'Aren't you writing today?' she asked testily, when it became clear he was in no hurry to leave even though he had finished his tea.

'Like I said,' he replied smoothly, 'you disturb my thoughts. I'm taking a well earned break.'

'But why come here?' she asked. 'Why seek me out?'

'I feel sorry for you,' he said surprisingly. 'Poor gullible little you, taken in by smooth-talking Eric. I thought you'd like to see something of the island before you go back.'

'I don't believe it,' she scoffed. '*You*, offering to take me—why?'

He shrugged and pulled a wry face. 'Let's say you intrigue me.'

'Or could it be that you're attempting to turn the tables on Eric?' she snapped. 'It occurs to me that you might think it funny to try and take me from him. It won't work. I love him, despite what you've told me, and I know when I get back I shall find out it's all a lie.'

He lifted his broad shoulders. 'You're a funny creature. Smart, seductive, self-assured, on the outside—but inside nothing but a mixed-up kid.'

'I'm not a kid!' replied Cathy angrily. 'I'm nineteen, quite old enough to know what I'm doing and to understand the ways of men like you.'

'Like me?' His mocking smile was very much in evidence. 'I'm willing to bet that you haven't been out with anyone like me before?'

She hadn't, that was true. Grant Howard was different—a man set apart from all others, and he knew it, that was the worst part about it. If he set out to take her from Eric, seduce her even, there was little she could do.

No woman in her right mind would turn him down. He was a sensuous male animal with an ability to arouse a woman's emotions merely by looking at her with those tawny eyes which could laugh or be serious, go light or dark, in a fraction of a second. They were laughing at her now, teasing, mocking, their light flecks very much in evidence.

Shivers ran down Cathy's spine and she turned her head quickly. He knew what he was doing to her, and he knew that she knew it too.

She stood up abruptly. 'I think it's time you went, Grant.'

'Why?' he asked lazily. 'Is there something you want to do?'

'No,' she replied quickly, adding mentally, 'I just want to get away from you. I can't stand you near me. I want to leave the island now, before it's too late.' But she knew she couldn't. The only thing she could do was keep away from Grant.

It would have been easy had he not chosen to seek

her out. Why? she asked herself once again. Why had he come? What was he trying to do?

'You're not taking me up on my offer, then? You don't want to see the island? A few hours by oxcart. It's beautiful, Cathy. It's the most beautiful island in the whole world.'

'And it belongs to you,' she snapped savagely. 'Is that what you're trying to tell me? It belongs to you and you'll never sell it, never. I'm wasting my time here.'

His eyes widened. 'You mean you did come to try and persuade me to sell?'

'No, no,' she said quickly, 'I didn't mean that. I meant it would be wasting my time looking at it when it can never belong to me. You're right, it is a beautiful place, but if I can't have it I don't particularly want to see it.'

Thick brows rose disbelievingly. 'You're telling me lies, Cleopatra. Is it because it's me who's offered to take you? If it was anyone else you'd gladly accept, is that it?'

She took the tray into the kitchen without answering, half expecting him to follow, relieved when he didn't. Back out on the terrace he said, 'You haven't answered my question. Why don't you want to come with me?'

'Because,' she said slowly, 'I would feel guilty knowing I was keeping you away from your precious work.'

'That's stupid,' he said harshly. 'I stopped writing of my own free will, not because of you, not because of anyone.'

'You said earlier that I disturbed you?' The moment the words were out she wished she could retract them. It sounded as though she had been flattered by his admission.

'Writers get mental blocks sometimes. Let's say it's one of those. Are you coming or not?'

He was looking up at her from his chair. Suddenly he caught her wrist and pulled her down on to his lap. Contact was explosive and Cathy knew then that she was going to say yes. This man had the most devious methods.

'Okay, I'll come,' she said hurriedly, rising to her feet, amazed when he let her go.

There was a smile on his lips which suggested that he knew he had won. Cathy felt like knocking it off, striking him across the face with all the force she could muster, but knew it would get her nowhere.

Grant still wore jeans, a clean pair today, though well worn, and his vest-like top moulded his superbly muscular chest, hiding none of his strength. His tan was deep, deep as mahogany, and he looked as though he would be more at home wielding a pick or shovel than tapping the keys of a typewriter.

He rose as soon as she accepted, smiled down into her eyes. 'Thanks, Cleopatra. The oxcart should be here any minute.'

She looked at him sharply. 'You'd already arranged it?'

'But of course. I knew you'd accept.'

His complacency angered her and she kicked his ankle viciously. He frowned, his face darkening, but she doubted whether it had hurt him. It had probably hurt her more; she had forgotten she wore open-toed sandals.

'I'll get my bag,' she said quickly, disappearing into

the chalet. She was still at a loss to understand why he had asked her out, but it would be churlish to refuse. She pushed a few things into her bag and when she returned the cart was there.

Grant was already sitting in it. He leaned down and gave her his hand, pulling her up easily and effortlessly. When she would have sat opposite he dragged her to the seat beside him.

She sat down, their bodies dangerously close. The oxcart moved away and they began their trip.

Despite her feeling of antagonism Cathy was entranced by it all—by the old planters' houses built on pillars above the ground, by the differing species of birds with their colourful tropical plumage, the exotic vegetation, the wide coralline roads, and the sweeping beaches on the other side of the island.

She already had on her bikini beneath her cotton dress and they swam in the clear, warm blue waters, laughing and shouting, splashing each other, playing as though they were lovers.

Lying on the sand afterwards Cathy was intensely aware of Grant at her side and the fact that his thigh brushed hers. An electric current ran through her and it was all wrong. Wrong, because she was in love with Eric. Wrong because this man was her enemy. He had told her stories about Eric that she did not wish to hear.

Suddenly she sprang to her feet. 'Don't you think it's time we went back? That poor man in the oxcart, he must be fed up.'

'He's used to it,' drawled Grant lazily. 'Come on, lie down again.'

Cathy shook her head. 'I want to go back to my chalet. I've had enough for today.'

'I see.' His eyes narrowed dangerously. 'You've had enough of my company, is that it?'

More than was good for her, she thought. He was too sensually attractive for her peace of mind and she wanted to escape his presence before she gave away her true feelings.

She was convinced now that he was attempting to attract her away from Eric. He wanted her to see that Eric really was not the man for her, that she had made a big mistake, that he was using her, but above all that she had no love for him.

Grant was going to try and make her fall in love with *him*. And it would be so easy. He was far more attractive than Eric, in a different kind of way. He was not so handsome, but there was something about him, a charisma, an all-powerful projection of his personality, that no one could deny.

If he chose to exert himself to win round anyone he could do it, she knew that, and this was his aim now—and she was falling for it, unable to help herself, completely aware of what was happening but without the power to stop it.

As they approached the Hotel Orange he said to her, 'How would you like to come and have dinner with me again tonight?'

With an attempt at aloofness she replied, 'No, thank you. I have other things to do.'

He frowned. 'Don't lie, Cathy. You know no one on the island apart from me, you have no excuse. You're coming and that's that.'

'I am?' she asked indignantly. 'No one orders me about!'

'Then accept,' he said tersely. 'It's that simple. I want your company, I want you tonight.'

Cathy stared, no one had ever spoken to her like this before. He wanted her, did he? In what way? She wanted him, her whole body and soul ached for him, was it in this way that he meant?

She found it hard to believe what was happening to her. Did people really fall in love just like that? Or was it purely physical attraction she felt?

She loved Eric, didn't she? How could she love Grant as well? The more she thought about it the more confused she became. Eric paled into insignificance beside Grant, so much so that it was easy to forget him while she was with the other man. Grant dominated her thoughts whether she liked it or not, and if she refused to go with him now she knew that he was quite capable of picking her up and carrying her.

'Why?' she objected loudly. 'Why me, when you made it so clear yesterday that you wanted to be on your own? You already surprised me by turning up here, now you want to further our acquaintance. I wish I understood your reasoning.'

He smiled mysteriously. 'Dear Cleopatra, you're irresistible, didn't you know that?'

She guessed he was teasing, but suddenly she didn't care. What did it matter? She could handle him, couldn't she? So why not? Why not make the most of what was being offered?

Her decision must have reflected on her face, for Grant said, 'I'm glad you've agreed to come. I've been without company for so long that I'm beginning to feel uncivilised.'

She could have told him that he looked it, with his unkempt hair and unpressed jeans, but she didn't. Instead she went inside to change.

She chose a simple short evening dress. What had

made her pack it, she did not know, but now she was glad. Perhaps she had subconsciously hoped that something like this might happen.

It was in a soft baby pink which suited her dark complexion. Grant looked at her closely, but said nothing, much to her disappointment.

Together they climbed the hill. It was not until they got inside that the real reason behind his invitation revealed itself.

'My housekeeper couldn't come today,' he said apologetically. 'Would you mind cooking dinner?'

CHAPTER THREE

CATHY glared angrily at Grant. 'Of all the devious, underhanded, lowdown methods—Grant Howard, I hate you!'

He laughed. He had clearly known what her reaction would be and was deriving great amusement from it.

'Get your own dinner,' she snapped. 'I'm going back to the hotel. I'm on holiday, remember?'

But he was at the door before she could open it. 'Dear Cleopatra, I'm sure you can cook as good as you look. Won't you do me this one favour?'

'You accused Eric of using people,' she cried, 'yet you're doing precisely the same. Let me go, this instant!'

Grant stood his ground and smiled, a sinister, mocking smile, and she knew she would not escape until she had done as he asked.

'You could have told me I was to be head cook before I changed,' she stormed, her blue eyes flashing belligerently.

'I can lend you a shirt and jeans,' he suggested amicably, still with that irritating grin.

'No, thanks, just an apron.'

'Search the kitchen,' he shrugged. 'I expect Mrs P.'s got one somewhere. Can I leave you to it while I get myself washed and changed? Seeing you in all your finery makes me feel guilty.'

Cathy sniffed. 'As if you'd care, but if I have to

cook dinner then I'd rather be alone. What do you want?'

'I'll leave you to it,' he said easily. 'I'm not fussy.'

Before she could say anything else he had gone. She could hear him running lightly up the stairs, singing to himself. He was happy about the situation; she wasn't. He had tricked her, and although she liked cooking she objected to being ordered to do it.

The kitchen, though, in this big house was beautiful, fitted with every modern convenience. It would be a pleasure working here—provided he kept his word and left her alone.

Cathy found an apron, a voluminous affair which covered most of her dress and reached well below her knees. She was glad there wasn't a mirror. She must look a sight!

She would have liked to cook an exotic dish, show him what a good cook she was; instead she decided on something simple that she knew would not go wrong, and an hour later they were sitting eating.

Grant had changed out of his denims into a pair of white slacks with prefect creases, and a black shirt, the sleeves rolled up to reveal powerful sinewy arms. His dark curly hair was still wet from the shower, brushed neatly into place, but already springing forward around his collar.

A few grey hairs glistened; she hadn't noticed them before. It added something, made him more attractive, more distinguished. She wouldn't have known him for the same man. He looked more like the image she had seen on the back of his book.

Only his big broad hands belied the fact that he might be a writer. They didn't fit the part. She could not imagine him pounding away on the keys of a typewriter. They looked too big, too clumsy. Yet when they had touched her that first time, when they had slipped inside her top, they had been incredibly tender and gentle, expertly drawing from her a response. He had known what he was doing. Those hands might be big, but they certainly weren't clumsy.

For starters they had melon and after that steak with chipped potatoes, mushrooms and fried tomatoes. Cathy had also managed to make a flan filled with fresh fruit.

Grant opened a bottle of red wine, a heady sweet mixture which teased her palate and made her head feel like cotton wool. She wondered whether he knew what he was doing, whether he had purposely chosen this wine knowing it was stronger than the one they had drunk last night.

She began to feel that she couldn't care less, that this evening was going to be enjoyable after all. Grant complimented her on her cooking, although he did laughingly accuse her of being conservative.

She did not offer to wash up, she thought she had done enough. He helped her carry the dishes out into the kitchen and then they returned to the garden room. Grant slid open the windows and they walked on to the terrace and when he took her into his arms she was not surprised.

'Thank you for a lovely meal,' he said, and kissed her.

Cathy thought her heart was going to stop beating. For one long-drawn-out second she seemed poised in infinity and then it began pumping again rapidly, painfully against her breast.

She wound her arms round the back of his head, pulling his face close to hers, meeting his lips. She was breathing deeply now and wondered where all this might end. Not that it bothered her, she was living for the moment. Grant was offering what she wanted and she was going to take it, and to hell with the consequences.

Eric had sent her here, and he must have known what sort of a man Grant was. Perhaps he didn't care what happened, perhaps after all, all he did care about was the island. It seemed likely now that he had envisaged what might happen, knew Grant might be attracted to her and hoped she would be able to use her influence to get him to sell the island to Eric.

What he hadn't considered was the fact that she might fall in love with Grant and out of love with him —if that was possible. It occurred to her that the feelings she had felt for Eric, the ones she had thought were love, had been mere infatuation for a rich man, for the boss. It was not true love, never would have been. They wouldn't have been happy, she could see that now. It had taken this man here to make her realise it, but did she love Grant? Was this what was happening to her, or was this merely infatuation too? Another man taking notice of her, making her feel wanted.

Two years ago she had been engaged to a boy she had known all her life. Even that had fallen through. Was she destined to a life falling in and out of love? Was she fickle? Cathy felt bemused and because she could not understand what was happening she held Grant more tightly than before.

His kisses became possessive threatening to swamp her, but she did not care. She could hardly breathe, but she wanted him and whatever he did she had no intention of stopping him.

It was Grant himself who drew the line yet again. 'I think we've had enough,' he said quietly, and there was a tremor to his voice, as though something had happened to him too, as if he had felt things the way she had, and realised it was all more than a game, that something was happening to them.

She returned to the room and sat down, her legs weak, her heart still fluttering. She looked up at Grant and her face was pale. 'I'm sorry,' she said. 'I didn't mean to——'

'It's I who should apologise,' he said roughly. 'I had no intention of that happening. Shall we have another drink?'

He moved across the room and Cathy was able to draw a deep reviving breath. He did things to her, this man, that should never be allowed. She looked at the broad back, the powerful thighs, at the dark curly hair falling over the collar of his shirt. He was the most virile man she had ever met, and she wished she understood what game he was playing.

He handed her her drink, taking care that their fingers did not meet, and sat down on the other side of the room. He had placed a record on the turntable, but tonight it was not soft romantic music that filled the air, but raucous disco sound, a modern rock band, something which Cathy had no feeling for, but it was what they needed right now, something to break the spell that had built up between them.

When Grant suddenly excused himself and she was left alone in the room Cathy was too restless to remain seated, and found herself drawn to the row of books all written by him.

He was some man. His research had taken him to all corners of the world, below ground, to the bottom of the ocean and out into space. It was no wonder that it took him several years to research each book, she thought, he was so thorough, leaving nothing to chance.

She took one of his earlier books from the shelf, flicking through the pages, noticing his concise way of writing, easily able to identify it with the man himself now that she had met him.

There was another photograph on the back cover, a much younger Grant this time, but still with that arrogant profile. Her heart began to race again as she studied the picture and she held the book against her breast for a few breathless moments.

She was being foolish, she knew, but she couldn't help it. She studied the likeness again, examining every detail of his face, from the sensuous lips to the deep seeing eyes, the determined chin and the irrepressible, curling hair.

There was a caption beneath and suddenly a few words seemed to jump out and hit Cathy, sending her reeling backwards, all colour draining from her face.

Howard Grant's wife and child live in France while the author himself—— She read no more, she didn't have to. It was enough, enough to tell her that she was wasting her time here, that she ought to have known better than to think he was doing anything other than amusing himself at her expense.

Carefully she replaced the book and then walked out of the house. Back in her chalet she took off her dress and stood beneath a freezing cold shower, but she felt no different. The shock was still there. She felt numbed, ashamed, angry.

Emotions conflicted with each other and when she went to bed she lay staring at the ceiling, hardly knowing what to think. Why had Grant done this to her?

Why had he made her fall in love when he knew he could not return it? Was it a game to him, his way of teaching Eric a lesson for daring to send her out here?

She wanted to cry, but the tears would not come. 'Oh, Grant,' she mouthed soundlessly into the night. 'Oh, Grant, why? Please tell me why!'

There was still another day to be got through before the boat came to take her back. If only there was some way she could get in touch, some way she could make the boatman come today so that she could get away—away from this, away from everything, away from Grant.

The love she felt was like nothing she had ever experienced before. It was like a seed growing inside her. Even if she never saw him again it would go on growing and she would always think of him.

She would think of him as her lover, and then she would remember his wife, and she would feel hatred, but she wouldn't mean it because she would never be able to hate him, her love wasn't like that. It was a real tangible thing that she could reach out and touch, and she wanted him.

But despite all this she was determined not to see Grant again before she left Samora, and in case he came down to find out why she had run away without so much as a goodbye she set off on foot the next morning for the other side of the island.

She was desperately tired after her sleepless night, but she drove herself on, only allowing herself to sit and rest when her aching legs would carry her no further.

There were nowhere near so many people on this side of the island and Cathy was able to relax, relieved that she did not have to put on a face and pretend nothing was the matter, when in point of fact she felt as though the world had come to an end.

As the morning dragged on she began to feel hungry. Foolishly she had not stopped for any breakfast, had felt then that food would choke her, but now hunger pains added to her misery—and there was nowhere that she could buy anything to eat!

One thing was certain, she was not going to knock on any of the doors of the few bungalows that were scattered here, she was not going to risk coming up against another Grant Howard type—and she definitely had no intention of going back, in case she bumped into him!

She returned to the forest and pulled down a bunch of bananas. They were tiny, tinier than any she had seen in England, and when she began to eat she could not stop. Before she realised it she had eaten the whole bunch. She laughed at herself for being greedy, but they were so delicious, so different.

After that she found a mountain stream with clear trickling waters and she cupped her hands and drank from it. It was like nectar. Replete, she found a grassy hollow and lay down. Soon she was asleep.

Several hours later she became aware of someone standing over her, a hand on her shoulder. Her eyes fluttered open and she saw an elderly man with steely hair and piercing blue eyes.

He looked worried and she smiled. 'I'm all right,' she said. 'I've only been asleep.'

'Thank goodness,' he said expressively, 'but I'm afraid you've got sunburn. Come back with me, my wife has some cream.'

Cathy jumped to her feet and shook her head. 'It's all right, thanks all the same. But I have some oil at the hotel.'

But the man would not take no for an answer. 'I insist,' he said, and took her hand, leading her forward as though she were a child. To her surprise Cathy found herself going. It was easier than arguing and he seemed a kind old man. Her discovery about Grant had left her weak. Whatever happened now could be no worse.

The man introduced himself as Jonathan. He was an Englishman, and told her he had retired to Samora. His wife, Martha, a plump venerable woman, took Cathy immediately under her wing, smoothing a cool white lotion over her sunburnt face and arms.

She tutted as she worked. 'You poor silly child! What made you go to sleep in the sun?'

Cathy smiled wryly. 'I didn't sleep last night, it must have caught up on me.'

Martha clucked, puzzled. 'A young girl like you not sleeping? What's wrong, man trouble?'

Cathy shook her head halfheartedly and knew Martha did not believe her. She was grateful, accepting now a glass of ice-cold milk.

'Stay for supper,' said Jonathan, 'if you've nothing else to do. It's not often the wife and I have company. We'd love you here.'

Cathy looked from one to the other, saw their happy smiling, uncomplicated faces, and nodded. 'I'd like that.'

She helped Martha in the kitchen with the sandwiches and after a while was able to forget her troubles. She had lost her own parents when she was small and took an instant liking to this couple, felt almost she could confide in them. She needed someone to talk to. But it was all so new yet, she could not quite bring herself to begin.

Long after their meal was finished they sat talking and it was dark when Cathy said she must return. During the course of their conversation she had told them she was staying at the Hotel Orange, but had let them assume she was on holiday, fighting shy of admitting the real reason.

Jonathan offered to accompany her, but she refused, although she did say that she would call to see them again before she left Samora.

Long before she reached her chalet, though, Cathy's happiness died away. It was a pleasant walk across the island with a silver moon lighting her way, but memories of Grant came tumbling back and she knew that until she had left for good they would always be there.

Even when she was back in London she would not forget, but at least there would be nothing to remind her of him. Here it was so easy to visualise him—on the porch where he had sat yesterday, or looking up at the white house where he lived alone.

Where was his wife, she wondered—still in France? Perhaps they didn't live together any more. And his child, how old would he be now? Or perhaps it was a girl? Did Grant ever see them—was he divorced? These were not questions she could ask unless he volunteered the information himself.

Her head was reeling when she went to bed, but surprisingly she fell asleep almost immediately. It was not long before she was dreaming of Grant, tortuous dreams—each time he rejected her and she woke feeling, if possible, more tired than when she had gone to bed.

She packed her case and stood it on the porch in readiness for her departure. A ferry called at the island that morning, taking away the holidaymakers and bringing in a new influx. Cathy stood and watched it, wondered whether she ought to return now. But then she thought of the boatman Eric had organised, realised he would have a wasted journey, and her conscience pricked her.

After lunch he had said he would come. Just enough time to visit Martha and Jonathan again. She swung round as the boat disappeared and made her way across the island.

'We're so glad you've come,' said Martha, welcoming her warmly into their house. 'We thought you'd forget us—we know what young people are like. How's your sunburn?'

Cathy looked surprised. 'I'd forgotten all about it. It was good stuff you put on.'

Martha was watching her closely. 'You don't look happy. Are you sad to be leaving?'

'In a way,' replied Cathy noncommittally.

'Or are you missing your young man?' asked the older woman sagely, lifting up Cathy's hand and looking at the sparkling diamond. 'Can't think why he let a pretty young girl like you come here on your own. He must trust you, that's all I can say.'

Cathy liked Martha's outspokenness and almost felt sorry to be leaving. She ate her lunch at the hotel and then picked up her case without bothering to go back into the chalet. She walked down to the shore, refusing to look up at the white house—just in case, she told herself. In case of what? In case Grant might be looking? Hardly likely. He had made no attempt to contact her again. It was the end of her sweet interlude.

He had played with her emotions, probably knowing exactly what he was doing. She wished she could hate him for it, but it was difficult, loving him as she did.

Perhaps when she got back to London, to Eric, she could forget all that had happened here, except that her fiancé would want to know, wouldn't he? She hadn't thought much about that. He would ask how she had got on. He would wonder whether she had met Grant, and although he might not ask he would try to wheedle it out of her in a roundabout sort of way. He was good at that, good at getting to know about things without asking direct questions. He was good at evading the issue too, she thought, and surprised herself by the bitterness of her feelings.

Grant had done this to her. He had made her suspicious. A lot had happened in the two short days she had been here and it was all because of him. How she wished they had never met!

She waited and waited for the boat. She waited all afternoon and half the evening, until it slowly dawned on her that the boat was not going to come. Had she mistaken the day? But no, the man had definitely said today. She could have sat down and cried.

Now what? There were no other boats on the island; she had discovered that already. It was an isolated community, people came here because they wanted to shut themselves away from the outside world. There were no telephones. Mail was delivered and picked up by the three-weekly ferry.

A startling thought! It meant that she could be here for another three weeks. How she wished she had gone on that boat this morning. She couldn't stay here that long—it was impossible.

Her feet dragged as she made her way back to the

chalet. She dropped her case outside and opened the door, stopping short when she saw it occupied by a young couple with a baby.

'Excuse me,' she said, 'but this is my chalet. I think there must be some mistake.'

The couple looked at her in surprise and broke out into voluble French. Cathy understood enough to realise that they had been allocated this chalet this morning and that there was no way that they were going to move.

In desperation she went to the hotel reception. 'Look here,' she said angrily to the startled receptionist, 'there's someone in my chalet. Will you please get them out?'

'I'm sorry, Miss Nielson,' said the dusky-skinned girl, 'but there's no mistake. Your chalet was booked for three nights only.'

Cathy was stunned. 'Have you another one?'

The girl shook her head apologetically. 'It's the busy season. We're full up.'

'You have nowhere you can put me?' Cathy felt desperate.

'I'm sorry, no.'

'I was supposed to have been picked up today, but the boat never came. What am I going to do?'

The girl behind the desk shrugged indifferently, as if to say it was no concern of hers, more or less implying that if Cathy was stupid enough to get herself into this situation then she would have to get herself out of it.

Cathy suddenly thought of Martha and Jonathan. They were the only people she knew on the island, apart from Grant, of course. Perhaps they could help? It was worth a try.

The three-mile walk seemed much further with her heavy suitcase. It never entered her head to hire an oxcart, not until she was halfway there, and then it was too late.

It was dark by the time she arrived. She tapped on the door and they were a long time in answering. When they did they were in their nightclothes, but their startled faces soon turned into beams of welcome when they saw who their unexpected visitor was.

'Come in, come in,' said Jonathan at once. 'What's happened? We thought you'd gone.'

Cathy grimaced and sank down into the nearest chair. 'The boat didn't come,' she said wearily, feeling close to tears, 'and there's not another ferry for three weeks. I don't know what I'm going to do. The hotel's full up, I've nowhere to go, and——'

Martha looked at her husband and back at the crestfallen girl. 'What a pity we have only the one bedroom or you could stay with us, but you must stop tonight, if you can manage on the settee, and perhaps in the morning we'll be able to sort something out.'

It did not take her long to make up a bed and soon Cathy was asleep, her troubles temporarily forgotten. But immediately she awoke the following morning they came flooding back and she could not imagine what she was going to do.

There had to be some way of making contact with the outside world. No one in this day and age could be completely cut off from civilisation. But it would appear they were. So much for Eric's careful planning, she thought ironically. What had gone wrong? It was so unlike him. Normally everything he arranged ran on well-oiled wheels, with never a hitch along the way.

Over breakfast Martha said quietly, 'Jonathan and

I have an idea. We'll ask our son if you can stay with him.'

'Your son?' It was the first Cathy had heard of him. 'Does he live on Samora?'

Martha nodded. 'Jonathan will go and see him as soon as he's finished eating, won't you, Jonathan?'

Her husband nodded and disappeared shortly afterwards while the two women set to clearing the table and tidying the bungalow before his return.

'I didn't know you had a son here,' said Cathy conversationally. 'Do you see much of him?'

'Not as much as we'd like,' said Martha, 'but he's busy, you understand. He bought us this bungalow, though, and he makes sure we want for nothing. We can't grumble.'

He sounded a paragon of virtue, thought Cathy, the ideal son in fact, and she wondered whether he was married. She was on the point of asking when Jonathan returned.

'No problem,' he said brightly. 'He's quite prepared to help out—on one condition.'

Martha looked at him sharply. 'Trust him! What does he want?'

'Can you type?' asked Jonathan.

Cathy nodded, but failed to see the connection.

'He says he'll give you free board and lodging if you'll do some secretarial work for him.'

Martha was indignant, her round face red with annoyance. 'How could he? It's not often we ask him a favour. He has no right to even think of such a thing.'

'You know your son,' said her husband logically. 'He turns every situation to his advantage. Can't say I blame him.'

'What do *you* think?' asked Martha worriedly, looking across at Cathy. 'I feel terribly guilty; after all, it was my suggestion. I shall certainly give him a piece of my mind!'

Cathy smiled and tossed her dark hair prettily. 'Don't worry, Martha. I don't mind, really I don't. In fact I shall be glad of the work. Three weeks is a long time with nothing to do. I've no other friends here, as you know. What does he do, this son of yours?'

Before either of them could answer the door burst open and whoever Cathy had expected it had certainly not been Grant Howard. She stared at him now in absolute horror, wishing that the floor would open and swallow her up.

Grant too was surprised, although he recovered more quickly. Looking across at Jonathan he said, 'I wish you'd told me it was Cleopatra. I would certainly not have been so willing to have her in my house.'

CHAPTER FOUR

GRANT had certainly made it clear that Cathy was unwelcome, but whether it was because she had run out on him or whether he too had had regrets about the incident that had taken place, she had no way of knowing. All she knew was that he was staring at her as though she was abhorrent to him, and she herself was rooted to the spot in a kind of shocked horror.

His parents frowned and Martha said, 'Cleopatra? Who are you talking about? Have you two met?'

Grant's eyes were enigmatic. 'You could say that. She came and asked me for a drink of water the other day. Broke a pile of glasses while she was at it.'

Martha laughed. 'Is that all? My goodness, Grant, there's no need to make so much fuss. You can certainly afford some more.'

'It wasn't that,' cut in Cathy tensely. 'It was because I interrupted him. You more than anyone should know that the genius doesn't like being disturbed.'

Grant's face hardened and she knew that had it not been for his parents' presence he would not have let her get away with that so easily.

Martha pretended not to hear, though she was clearly disturbed by the positive hatred between her son and the young girl she had taken into her home. 'Why didn't you tell me, Cathy, that you knew Grant?'

'I didn't know myself until he walked in. I'd no idea. You never mentioned his name.' She could not help wondering whether Grant would retract his offer of help now that he knew who she was. On the one hand she wished he would—it would be an impossible situation, yet on the other hand she needed him; there was absolutely nowhere else for her to go.

She was stranded here on Samora without a roof over her head and with no other friends than Grant's parents. She wouldn't class him as a friend. An acquaintance, perhaps, an intimate acquaintance even, but someone with whom she had no wish to further a relationship.

Martha chose to ignore the tension and said approvingly, 'I'm glad you two have met, it will make things easier all round. But don't work her too hard, Grant. She looks fragile to me.'

Grant said harshly, 'You know what my terms are.'

His mother looked outraged and his father frowned. Cathy said, 'I wouldn't dream of coming to live with you under any other circumstances, Mr Howard. I'm quite an efficient secretary, I hope I shall be able to please you.'

'Me too,' came the abrupt reply. 'Are you ready?'

'Won't you stay for a cup of tea?' begged his mother, still hoping, thought Cathy, to ease the tension between them.

Grant shook his head crossly. 'I'm busy. The oxcart's waiting. Come along, Cathy.'

His mother shrugged and looked hopelessly at the younger girl. 'I'm sorry,' she whispered, 'but he's a nice boy really.'

Cathy could not help smiling, particularly as Grant had heard his mother's hushed words and was even more furious than before.

She climbed into the cart unaided. Grant did not even lift a finger to help, and even if he had she would have ignored it. She took her case from his father and sat stiffly on the edge of the seat, waving goodbye, smiling brightly as though she was going on some wonderful journey.

During the winding tortuous ride up to the white house Grant remained silent, and Cathy wondered whether after all it was a wise thing she had done. No doubt if she had gone to him for help in the first place, instead of his parents, he would have refused. It was only the fact that they had asked on her behalf that had made him agree. Even so she would have liked to bet that had he known who she was he would still have said no.

It surprised her that he looked like neither of his parents. Martha was round and cuddly and soft, and Jonathan, although of equal height, was nothing like his son. Grant was an individual, an immensely strong character who had developed in his own way. They must be proud of him, she thought, proud of his success, the status it had given him.

It was quite clear that they respected his privacy and unlike most parents were not given to popping in to see him at all hours of the day.

As soon as they reached the house Grant disappeared, leaving Cathy standing in the black and white tiled hall. For a good ten minutes she stood there not knowing what to do. Suddenly footsteps sounded and a thin grey-haired woman appeared with a long sharp nose and beady eyes and a forbidding expression on her mean face.

The housekeeper, thought Cathy, and for some reason she doesn't approve of me.

'Miss Nielson, come with me, please,' and Cathy

had no alternative but to follow her clacking heels up the wide marble staircase and along the red-carpeted corridor.

At the end the housekeeper stood back for her to enter. Cathy dropped her suitcase inside the door and stepped into the room. Compared with the palatial splendour of the rest of the house it was spartan.

A bed with a white cotton throwover stood in one corner. The bare boards were not relieved by even the tiniest of carpets, the walls white and simple and unadorned. A tiny window looked out at the mountainside rising steeply above them and she almost expected to see bars at the windows.

But she supposed she must be thankful, at least she had a roof over her head. The housekeeper disappeared and Cathy was left wondering whether it had been Grant's idea that she was put into this room, or whether the mean-looking woman had taken it upon herself.

Mrs P., he had called her. Mrs Prim, thought Cathy disrespectfully. It was clear she hated the intrusion and Cathy wondered why—because it made more work, or did she regard herself as Grant's bodyguard endeavouring to ward off all members of the opposite sex?

She had no need to worry so far as Cathy was concerned. Cathy had come here to work and work she would. She had no wish for any further entanglement with Grant. There could be no satisfying end to such a relationship, only more heartache. The wisest course would be to remain aloof, do as he asked and keep herself to herself.

Three weeks was not so long. Or was it? Two days

had seemed an age; three weeks was a lifetime. And then there was Eric to consider. He would wonder what had happened to her.

Perhaps he would discover that the boatman had never turned up and send someone else out for her. Perhaps she ought to leave a message at the hotel. But when she thought how he had deceived her she changed her mind. Let him worry! It would serve him right for getting her out here under false pretences.

She sighed and began emptying her case. Once her dresses were hung behind a curtain in one corner, and her underwear put away in the drawers, she made her way back downstairs.

She did not know which room was Grant's study. She did not even know whether he would want her to interrupt him, or whether she ought to wait until he came to find her.

But she couldn't stand here all day, could she? she argued, so slowly she walked along the corridor, listening carefully at each door. Once she thought she heard papers rustling and listened more intently for a few seconds.

Suddenly the door was flung wide and Grant stood there, a thunderous frown creasing his forehead. 'What the hell are you doing?' he demanded.

'I wasn't prying, if that's what you think,' retorted Cathy. 'I was trying to find out which was your study. I'm here to help, in case you'd forgotten.'

'The normal practice is to knock, not listen at keyholes,' came the biting reply.

What had happened to the Grant she had learned to love? she asked herself painfully. This was the Grant she had first met, the man she hated. He had two sides to his character, and it became apparent that this one was the one she was going to see the most of.

It was preferable, she argued with herself. As a matter of fact, it was the only way. If he was nice to her she would not be able to work in close proximity without giving away her true feelings.

'I suppose you'd better come in,' he said reluctantly at length, and turned back into the room. All was chaos, at complete variation with the rest of the house.

Cathy's horrified eyes surveyed the littered desk and open books, a tape recorder with the tape spilling out on to the floor like a tangled ball of wool. Grant had clearly been having difficulties, and she could not help an inward smile at the thought of things not going quite right for this smug man.

She wondered what it was he wanted her to do. There looked to be enough work to keep someone busy for a lifetime. The filing cabinet had piles of papers on the top, drawers half open, files pulled out. It certainly needed organising. He might be a good writer, she thought, but he was not a very orderly one.

She had not realised that he was watching her, or that her face had given her away, until he said, 'Okay, so I'm not the world's tidiest person, but there's no need to look so distasteful. Is the work going to be too much for you, is that what you're thinking?'

Cathy shook her head hurriedly. 'Not in the least. I was merely wondering how you could work in such a mess.'

He frowned angrily. 'It might surprise you, but I know exactly where everything is. I've had people like you here before, tidying up around me, and then once they've gone I've never been able to find anything.'

'Perhaps your system needs updating,' she said

politely. 'If things were filed properly you should have no difficulty.'

'Do you think you'll be able to do that?' he sneered, 'in three short weeks, without any form of disaster?'

He had thrown out a challenge and Cathy grasped it with both hands. 'I've no doubt that I could, if you give me free rein.'

He snorted derisively. 'That's something I'm not prepared to give. The book I'm working on at the moment is taboo. I want nothing connected with it touched by you. I don't allow anyone to see my work before it's published.'

Cathy shrugged indifferently. 'Okay, so you tell me what I'm not to touch and I'll sort out the rest.' She hoped she sounded efficient, she was not really feeling it. This man made her feel inferior—but she could not stop the love bubbling over inside!

Each time she looked at him a tremor passed through her and her heart pounded at an alarming rate. She was so sure that he must be aware of it that she refused to look at him, picking up a paper here, glancing at a file there, anything to avoid meeting his eyes.

'God damn you, woman,' he snapped, 'look at me when I'm speaking! Are you afraid of me or something?'

She squared her shoulders, forcing herself to forget that there was another Grant she knew and loved. This was the man she was to work with, this bad-tempered, unapproachable character, and she would be as well to remember it.

'Why should I be afraid of you?' she asked defiantly, bravely staring back into his face.

The golden eyes blazed down on her. She felt almost crushed beneath their intensity and put her hand to her throat, choking back a panicky cry.

'Where would you like me to start?' she enquired tentatively, her voice quavering. At that moment she would have liked nothing better than to turn tail and run, but she knew this was what he expected, that he would be a hard taskmaster, determined to break her for reasons known only to himself. It was there in his eyes; he didn't want her here he had only done it to please his parents, and he would do everything in his power to get rid of her without actually going to the extreme of throwing her out.

He pointed towards the cabinet. 'You can make a start there.' His decision made, he turned his back on her, sitting down at his desk and beginning to type.

For a few seconds Cathy watched. His broad fingers touched the keys lightly. He typed faster than any woman, faster than herself, and she could not help admiring him.

Already he was in a world of his own, had forgotten she was there. She felt that she could have walked up to him, touched the springing curly hair, kissed his nape, even, and he would not have noticed, so immersed was he in his work.

With a little sigh she turned and crossed to the cabinet, fighting back the tears which pricked her eyes. A filing clerk was what he had relegated her to. It wasn't a secretary he wanted, he obviously had every intention of doing all the typing himself. There had been little point in asking whether she could type. He merely wanted a general office clerk, someone to tidy up after him.

She had hoped, when Grant said he needed a secretary, that she might help in typing out his books. It would have been interesting, it would have given her an insight into his character, told her a little about himself, the way he ticked; because she was quite sure it was impossible to write a book without part of the author creeping into it.

Time and time again she turned away from the cabinet and looked across at Grant, but he was oblivious to her, pushing himself, working hard, typing fast and furious—and accurate, she had no doubt.

Looking through the files she was able to see exactly why he had difficulty in finding anything he wanted. The whole system was simply A to Z. Anything beginning with the letter A was filed under it, anything from aeroplane to antelope. The files were bulging and to find any one letter, or any one article, any piece of research, would take an absolute age. Each file needed splitting up into several headings.

It was a mammoth task, yet a necessary one. There was a table near the window littered with what she presumed was more filing. Cathy piled them on to one side and then took out the first file.

Very painstakingly and methodically she began to sort them out into different groups. She found a box containing new folders and set out her subject headings, slipping each paper into the appropriate file as she came to it. It took her the whole of the morning to do the letter A.

At this rate, she thought, it will take me a fortnight to do this cabinet alone. No wonder Grant had scoffed when he'd said he thought the work might be too much for her. He had known what was involved.

Nevertheless she was determined to succeed, and had it not been for the housekeeper announcing lunch she would have been prepared to work through until whatever time Grant suggested they call it a day.

He frowned at the interruption, nodding briefly towards Mrs P. and carried on with his typing. Cathy didn't know what to do. She was hungry, but felt that perhaps he was setting the pace and wouldn't approve if she went and ate her lunch leaving him working.

In the end common sense prevailed. She would get on much better this afternoon if she had a break. If Grant wanted to work, let him, she didn't care.

She followed the housekeeper to the dining room where a pine table was set for two. A bowl of salad stood in the centre and a plate of smoked salmon to one side. It looked positively delicious and Cathy ate with relish.

When she had finished she wondered whether she ought to remind Grant about lunch. The fact that Mrs P. had knocked on his door suggested that he normally ate, so why had he not come today? Was it because of her? She was torn between fetching him or loading a tray and taking it in.

A tray on the sideboard made up her mind for her. She arranged it carefully and carried it into his study. He did not appear to hear her enter, but when she slid the tray on to his desk, moving a few papers to make room for it, he stopped typing and gave his customary harsh frown, his eyes scraping her face.

'What the hell?'

'Your lunch,' she said, trying hard to maintain an imperturbable air.

'I'm not hungry,' he growled.

'You must eat,' she insisted. 'You'll work better if you do.'

'You sound like my mother,' he flicked. 'I can't stand people who fuss. Go away!'

Cathy backed obediently, his angry words catching her on the raw. Biting her lip, she returned to her filing.

It was interesting, actually. There were a lot of boring letters, but there was also a lot of his research. She already knew that he was a very thorough man, but had not realised exactly how much work he put into each of his novels.

It was all here, and she intended filing them very very carefully and very very accurately, so that if ever Grant needed to refer to any of it again he would have no difficulty in finding anything at a glance. He would remember her, if only for her capabilities as a filing clerk, she thought wryly.

Glancing back across the room, she saw that he was eating and had poured a second cup of coffee. She smiled to herself.

When he had finished she took the tray. She had expected thanks, but didn't get it. He had once more gone back to his typing and she might as well not have been there.

The day passed quickly after that. Cathy became so immersed in her work that she even managed to forget Grant. It was not until he himself declared it was time to stop that she realised it was almost seven.

'Your time's your own now,' he said tersely. 'Mrs P. will have gone, but I've no doubt she's left dinner. Help yourself, I'm going out.'

It was on the tip of Cathy's tongue to ask where, but she stopped herself just in time, knowing he would never answer such a question. She wondered whether he had a girl-friend on the island.

He was a strange man, and the more time she spent with him the less she understood him.

Once again she ate a solitary meal, and then afterwards, unable to bear the loneliness of the house, she walked down the hill and made her way to his parents' bungalow.

They were pleased to see her, asking many questions as to how her first day had gone. 'Grant popped in here an hour ago,' added Martha. 'We asked him, but he was noncommittal. Are you getting on all right?'

She was anxious, realised Cathy, in some strange way hoping that the two of them would get on together. Didn't it matter to her that her son was married, that somewhere in the world he had a wife and child?

Jonathan too appeared to be waiting for her answer, so Cathy smiled and nodded, tried to appear enthusiastic. 'Time's gone so quickly,' she said. 'I suppose it must prove that I'm enjoying myself. Grant's a very busy man.'

'Don't we know it!' sighed Martha resignedly. 'He works too hard. We tell him that, but he doesn't take any notice.'

'I doubt if he takes notice of anyone,' replied Cathy. 'He's a law unto himself.'

'You've discovered that already?' asked Jonathan with a wry smile.

'The day I first met him,' she answered ruefully.

'He wouldn't have liked you going up to his house and asking for a drink of water,' said his mother, 'and then breaking some glasses into the bargain. I can imagine his reaction!'

'It was rather a tense moment,' admitted Cathy. 'He wasn't at all happy.'

'I don't suppose he would be,' said the older woman. 'Grant likes his privacy, especially since——' She stopped suddenly, clamping up, as though regretting whatever it was she had been going to say.

'After what?' ventured Cathy timidly.

But Martha shook her head. 'Nothing. Have you eaten?'

Cathy nodded. 'I'd love a drink, though, if you're making one.' Clearly Martha was going to tell her nothing else, but she couldn't help wondering what she had been going to say. Something must have happened to make Grant shut himself away like this. Would she find out before she left, or would it be a perpetual mystery?

Martha looked at her husband. 'Be a dear, Jonathan, and put the kettle on.'

He did more than that; he made the tea while the two women talked, and later, much later, he walked her back to the bottom of the hill. He would have gone all the way, but Cathy insisted that it would be too much for him and that she was quite capable of finding her way alone.

'There's nothing to worry about,' she laughed. 'No poisonous snakes, no wild animals. No harm will come to me.'

He let her go reluctantly, but when she reached the house to find Grant waiting for her, an immediate, 'Where the devil have you been?' was thrust harshly at her, and she wished she hadn't been so adamant. With his father here Grant would never have dared speak to her like this.

She looked at him hostilely. 'I don't see that it's any business of yours, but if you must know, I've been to see your parents.'

He looked slightly mollified, but still angry. 'Next time you go out please leave a note.'

'Don't tell me you were worried,' scoffed Cathy. 'Surely you'd have been only too pleased if I hadn't come back. You made it quite clear in front of your parents that you weren't keen on having me. I know it's only for their sake that you've done it, so you needn't pretend that it's because of any feelings you might have. That little incident the other night—it was a try-on, wasn't it? See how far you could go. In case you're wondering, it meant nothing to me either. I'd already forgotten you when you turned up again this morning.'

'Then why did you run away, if it meant so little to you?'

'I decided it was time I went, that's all.' Cathy managed to hold his eyes so that he had no choice other than to believe she was telling the truth.

'If it really did mean nothing then you won't object if I repeat the experiment?' His eyes darkened ominously and Cathy should have been warned, but before she could anticipate his next move his arms had slid behind her back, pulling her inexorably against him, his mouth claiming hers possessively.

She fought furiously, fought her own instincts to respond, fought also his vice-like grip, but to no avail. She lost on both counts. Exactly why he was kissing her she had no idea, but after a while she ceased to care and gave herself up to the pleasure of the moment.

The interlude ended abruptly when he thrust her from him with a gesture of disgust. 'I didn't see you fighting,' he spat angrily.

'Neither did I return your embrace,' replied Cathy quickly. 'Your kisses leave me cold. You're wasting your time if you think you're going to get anywhere with me.' She wiped the back of her hand across her mouth as if to imply that she found his kisses distasteful.

Grant frowned savagely and pushing open his study door disappeared inside. It closed with a resounding thud.

Cathy wondered whether he was going to work—not that it mattered to her, but it wouldn't do his health any good, working all day and all night. But why should she care, she asked herself, after the way he'd treated her? Let him work himself into an early grave if he wanted to!

She went to bed, to her little bare room at the end of the corridor. But she couldn't relax, she found herself listening for his footsteps on the stairs. She knew that stupidly she would not rest until he too was in bed.

She had no fear that he might intrude on her privacy, no qualms that they were the only two people in the house, that didn't frighten her, but she did wish he would settle.

Had she herself done this to him? Was it the fact that he was sharing his house begrudgingly with her that made him so restless? He said he liked the privacy here, had she spoiled that? Was he regretting allowing her to come? Was she disrupting his life to such an extent that he would be unable to write? She would hate to do that to him, though judging by the way he had worked today it seemed hardly likely.

It was about three before she finally heard him, his feet moving slowly as though he was tired, and she would have liked nothing more than to go out and comfort him. But she knew she daren't, and soon afterwards she fell asleep, waking with a sense of shock the next morning to find that it was almost nine.

She jumped out of bed, angry with herself for not waking earlier; she had intended to be ready and working by now. Almost running into the bathroom, she washed and dressed quickly, hurrying downstairs, going straight to the study without bothering about breakfast.

Grant was already working, which surprised her, considering his late night. He did not bother to look up, nor even answer her polite, 'Good morning.'

She shrugged mentally and made her way to her desk, working silently and efficiently, but all the time aware of the man sitting only a few yards away from her.

By mid-morning Cathy was starving and knew she could work no more until she had eaten. She wondered whether the housekeeper had arrived, or whether it would be all right if she went into the kitchen and made herself a cup of coffee and a slice of toast.

She paused beside Grant's desk. 'Would you like a drink?' she asked hesitantly.

He glanced up impatiently, 'What?' and then as if suddenly realising what she had said, 'No, thanks,' and he was back at his work again. She guessed he had hardly noticed the interruption.

In the corridor she bumped into Mrs Prim carrying a tray with two cups of coffee and a plate of biscuits. Cathy smiled and attempted to take it from her. 'Just what we need,' she said brightly.

But the housekeeper neither returned her smile nor would relinquish the tray. 'I can manage,' she said tightly, and brushed past Cathy into the office, placing the tray on a side table, and leaving without another word.

Cathy picked up one of the cups and took it across to Grant, as well as the plate of biscuits. 'Won't you stop for five minutes?' she suggested timidly. 'I'm sure you must need refreshment after working so hard. I didn't expect you down so early when you were up half the night.'

He sighed deeply and his fingers stilled. 'When will you get it into your thick head that I abhor interruptions—and how do you know what time I went to bed, were you listening for me?'

To agree would be an admission that he had made an impression on her so Cathy shook her head. 'I couldn't sleep—a strange house, I suppose.'

'Or perhaps you were hoping that I would come into your room. Was that what you were after, Cleopatra? Despite the fact that you hastened to assure me that my kisses meant nothing were you after a companion to share your bed? Was that your idea all along? Was that why you inveigled your way into my house?'

Cathy curled her fingers into her palms to stop herself from hitting him. 'Had I known Martha and Jonathan were your parents,' she said distantly, 'I would certainly have never gone along with their suggestion that they ask their son to help out. Nothing would have persuaded me to share this house with you.'

'Yet you still came. Why, I wonder? It would have been easy to refuse, once you'd discovered my identity.'

Cathy shrugged. 'I didn't want to hurt your parents.'

'You seem to have grown rather attached to them.'

'Is that any crime?' she returned crisply. 'They're a

nice couple, friendly and welcoming. More than I can say for their son!'

She expected an angry retaliation, was surprised when he finished his coffee and carried on with his typing without so much as another word. Only a telltale pulse jerking in his jaw told her that he was angry —but she didn't care. He deserved it. He *was* unwelcoming. He was the most anti-social person she had ever met!

During the next few days Cathy became accustomed to this pattern of procedure. They would work all day, rarely speaking, and when they did, it was to argue. In the evenings Grant would go out. He never told her where he was going, but he never came back late, usually about half past ten. By then Cathy would be in bed, having grown bored with her own company.

She had taken to reading his books, could almost say that she had become a Howard Grant fan, and it was not difficult to imagine him actually living the part of some of his heroes, particularly the one who became a mercenary. It would suit him perfectly.

So far as the filing was concerned she was disappointed that Grant had never once asked her how she was getting on, or even come across to see what she was doing. He did not even know that she was revamping the system. She hoped he would approve, it would be too late afterwards if he didn't.

Her love for him was growing daily, a desperate kind of love that she tried to push to the back of her mind. But working together day by day, talking to him, watching him, aching for him, it was an impossibility.

The nights were the worst, long lonely nights lying in her hard narrow bed, knowing that he was only a few doors away. She had never seen his room but could imagine it to be the utmost in luxury, as were all the other rooms in the house. Precisely why she had been given this barren room she did not know, but she did know that she would never complain, never give Grant the opportunity to tell her to go if she was not satisfied.

Sometimes she would spend an hour with his parents, but not too often in case they guessed things were not running as smoothly between her and Grant as they would have liked. She had no wish for them to question Grant. He would think she had been telling tales behind his back, and she would never do that, she loved him too dearly.

It was Wednesday morning when Cathy found Grant standing over the filing cabinet, apparently waiting for her, papers scattered all over the place.

An angry scowl darkened his brow. 'Where the hell's that research I did on Cornish tin mines?'

'That would depend on where it was originally filed,' she replied reasonably, trying hard to keep her temper, which was difficult in the face of his antagonism. 'I've split each file into separate headings. I've done C and it certainly wasn't under that. Would it be under M for mines, do you think, or T?'

Grant's scowl deepened and she knew he was of the opinion that she was having a go at him. But she wasn't. To her it was a perfectly reasonable question.

'How the devil should I know?' he rasped. 'I just shove everything on one side and leave it to my so-called secretaries to sort out.'

And if you treat them all like this, thought Cathy, it's no wonder you never get anywhere! She doubted whether any of them would stop for more than half a day.

She picked up the file marked M and carefully leafed

through the contents, but she could not see anything remotely connected with tin mines.

Grant was growing more and more impatient and when she picked up the T file he snatched it from her and riffled through the papers himself, caring little that half of them spilled to the floor.

Eventually he found what he was looking for, dropped the rest down on to her desk, oblivious to the fact that he scattered papers Cathy had carefully sorted the day before.

Without stopping to think she said hotly, 'There's no need for that, Grant. I'm doing the work as quickly as I can, and I've not even had so much as a thank you.'

He glanced at her harshly. 'If it's thanks you're after you're in the wrong place. You're merely earning your keep. What else do you expect?'

'A little civility, that's what,' she snapped.

His head jerked. 'Politeness is not one of my strong points, as you've obviously gathered. Don't forget it wasn't my idea you came here.'

'Are you telling me I should go?' she demanded angrily, her blue eyes flashing sparks of ice. What a perfectly loathsome man he could be at times! How could she possibly love him?

He lifted one eyebrow mockingly, his tawny eyes gleaming directly into her own. 'You can please yourself what you do.' But he knew as well as she that until the next ferry came there was no way that she could get off the island.

She was virtually a prisoner. The whole island was a prison really. Everyone on it had to plan their moves three weeks ahead. There could be no hasty decisions, it had to be predetermined every time.

She supposed that normally it worked very well, but

in the case of illness, what then? Okay, so there was a doctor on the island and a cottage hospital of sorts, but what if anyone was seriously ill?

She had given up trying to work out this problem ages ago, but Grant saying this to her now made her think again. She would not have been surprised if a man of his means had a helicopter hidden away somewhere so that he could come and go as he pleased. It was difficult to imagine Grant relishing the thought of being imprisoned here for weeks at a time, only able to leave when the ferry came.

Returning her attention to the papers on her desk, Cathy gave an impatient sigh. She intended doing a cross-referenced index to the whole system when it was completed, so that Grant would never have any difficulty in finding anything he wanted. It was only at this intermediate stage that things were difficult.

If he had asked her for the papers in the first place instead of ploughing through everything, ruining all her careful work! Furious anger ran through her and she felt like picking up a file and slinging it at the back of his head. Would it make her feel any better? she asked herself.

Yes, it would, urged a demon inside, and without more ado Cathy picked up a file and flung it with all her strength.

Unfortunately, instead of hitting him, it landed on the pile of papers at the side of his typewriter, and the work he had been doing for days and days went flying across the room.

She could not have made him more angry had she tried. He rounded on her in a roar, his face suffused with dark anger, his hands outstretched as though he would like to strangle her. She had seen him in a temper, but nothing like the one he was in now.

'My God, I'm sorry,' she cried before he could speak. 'I didn't mean to do that.'

'I know damn well what you meant to do,' he growled. 'It was me you aimed at. You did it once before, but that time you hit me. Pity you weren't such a good shot today.'

She bit back an angry retort. 'I'll pick them up for you, I really am sorry.'

When he rasped harshly that he would do it himself she remembered that he liked no one to see his work at this stage.

'It's all right,' she said quickly, 'I won't read it, if that's what's worrying you,' and she knelt down beside him.

She had expected that he would push her away, that he would send her flying across the room. She even tensed herself in readiness, but to her surprise he allowed her to gather up the papers.

His close proximity caused her heartbeats to quicken until they felt like a drum in her ears. She wondered whether he could hear, whether the faint flush staining her cheeks was a giveaway, or whether, if he noticed, he would think it was because she was embarrassed about spilling his papers.

When they were eventually all picked up she tried to take them from him. 'Please let me sort them for you.'

His fingers tightened. 'I can manage.'

'You're being silly,' she said crossly, recklessly. 'You have a phobia about people seeing your work. What the blazes do you think I'm going to do, copy from you? You go on about me wasting your time, but surely it would help now if I did this while you get on with your book?'

He looked at her suspiciously for a few long seconds. 'Maybe you're right,' came the grudging reply, and he allowed her to take the papers from him, over to her own desk near the window.

It did not take her long to put them back into numerical order, but it was impossible not to read a few of the lines as she did so. She tried not to, appreciating his desire for secrecy, but it was surprising how the words seemed to jump out and hit her, just as had those few words on the back of the book when she had learned of his marriage.

It appeared that this novel was about a child who had grown up in a tug-of-love situation between his parents. From the few lines she read it was a very moving story and she had every confidence that it would be as successful as all his other novels.

It was different from the action-packed pages which were Howard Grant's normal style of writing, she could see that immediately. It was filled with pathos, human emotion and grief, a love tangle—and she could appreciate his sensitivity about anyone reading it.

Once the pages were collated she returned them to his desk. He nodded absent-mindedly and that was all the thanks she got. Not that she had really expected any, when it had all been her fault in the beginning.

But she felt strangely close to tears. It was getting harder and harder working for this man who did not appreciate her. She wondered whether in fact she was doing him a favour, or whether after she had gone his office would resume its former muddle.

It came very much as a surprise therefore when Grant announced that evening that he was not going out and she would have the pleasure of his company during dinner.

She could not help wondering whether his mother had said anything. Once or twice Martha had expressed disgust with her son for leaving Cathy alone in the big house every evening, only Cathy's insistence that she did not mind prevented her from tackling Grant. On the other hand, it was hardly likely that Grant would take any notice of anything his mother said. He did only what he wanted. What reason he had for staying in tonight she would never know, nevertheless she was grateful.

As she went upstairs to change Cathy found herself humming softly. It was the happiest she had felt since coming here. It was silly, really, they were sharing a meal, nothing more; for all she knew he might not even speak during the whole of the evening.

She changed into the pink dress she had worn on that fateful night. It brought back painful memories, but as it was the only evening dress she had packed she could do nothing about it.

When finally she went downstairs Grant was already in the dining room. He wore a cream evening suit which complemented his mahogany tan to perfection. He had never looked so attractive. His dark hair was combed close to his head, gone was the perpetual frown, and for once he set himself out to be the perfect host.

During the meal their conversation inevitably turned to his writing. Cathy discussed the several books of his which she had now read, and then, almost without thinking, asked how his current novel was progressing.

It was the wrong thing to say, she realised immediately she saw the change in his face. Gone was the easy camaraderie, his eyes became blank and he looked at her coldly. 'My book is my own affair, I thought I'd made that quite clear.'

Cathy lifted her shoulders in a half shrug. 'I'm sorry, I was merely trying to be polite. I had no intention of prying.'

'Well, don't,' he snapped. 'The topic is forbidden.'

'Suit yourself,' said Cathy, half to herself, half aloud, and he frowned even more strongly.

'You think I'm being unreasonable?'

'As a matter of fact I do.' Her pretty blue eyes were wide and hostile. 'I think you've been unreasonable over the whole affair of my being here.'

'As I never wanted you in the first place I don't see how you can say that.' He swallowed a mouthful of wine and stared at her coldly.

Cathy gritted her teeth. 'I consider I'm doing a fair day's work in exchange for a roof over my head and food in my stomach. You're the most ungrateful person I've ever come across, and if it wasn't for the fact that I have no option I wouldn't stay here a moment longer!'

Grant's nostrils flared and she could see his knuckles gleaming white as he held his knife and fork tighter. She had the feeling that he would have liked nothing better than to stab her with the knife. He had that look in his eyes, a wild, crazy look, and she could not imagine why their conversation had angered him so.

It was beyond her that he should regard his book so sacrosanct that he could not bear to discuss it. It was a very moving story and from what little she had read she knew that it had been written with great feeling—almost as though it was something he had gone through himself—but why guard it so zealously?

'Perhaps it would be better,' he said at length, 'if

you and I worked in separate rooms. It's become quite obvious to me that having you in my study is not going to work.'

Cathy felt like crying; he was shutting her out in more ways than one. 'Why?' she asked. 'Why, Grant? I've not noticed that my presence has stopped you from working. You seem to be getting on very well. You're hammering away at your typewriter for hours on end. I don't know how you do it. You don't seem to have to stop to think, the words simply flow.'

'Are you an authority on writing?' he demanded impatiently. 'You don't know the first thing about it. I'm not happy with anything I've done since you've been here. You disturb me.'

She disturbed him, did she? But not in the way she would have liked. Not in the way a woman disturbs a man to the extent that he wants to make love to her. This was how she reacted to him, and she would like nothing more in the world than for him to return these feelings.

Each time she thought of his coldness she felt sad, cut off. He had only once let himself go, and she could have sworn then that he was not as immune to her as he made out.

She wondered why he had drawn these shutters round himself, why he was rejecting her. But she would have to go on wondering; there was no way that she could ask, no way that her pride would let her admit that she loved him. When her three weeks were up she would go, and that would be the end of this bitter-sweet interlude.

She pushed her plate away, her food hardly touched, and stood up.

'Where are you going?' Grant demanded savagely.

'I can't eat any more,' she said. 'I'm suddenly not hungry.'

'The conversation too much for you?' he sneered, and then to her surprise he rose too, his face changing dramatically. 'Damn the food,' he said thickly, and pulled her into his arms. 'Is this the sort of food you want?' His mouth was dangerously close to hers. 'You've looked at me with your love-starved eyes all evening, is this what you're after?'

Had she really been so obvious? thought Cathy shamefully, while at the same time her breathing deepened and rising emotion threatened to choke her. She was almost afraid to look into his eyes and did not even cry out when he roughly caught a handful of hair and jerked back her head.

He covered her face with kisses, hot searing kisses, and Cathy closed her eyes against the passion she glimpsed briefly on his face. When his mouth covered hers in a harsh demanding kiss she was carried away on a tide of emotion and pressed herself against him, feeling the hardness of his thighs against her own, her breasts crushed against the iron muscles of his chest.

When he lifted her into his arms and carried her out of the room she thought for one brief ecstatic moment that he was going to take her to bed. Dutifully she began to struggle, but when his arms tightened like steel bands she lay still.

But it was not to his bedroom that he took her, it was the garden room. He laid her down on the deep-piled carpet and she moaned softly, holding up her arms, her lips parted expectantly, her blue eyes shining like jewels.

CHAPTER FIVE

GRANT towered over her like a giant, physically exciting, emotionally exhausting, and the only person she had ever wanted to possess her.

It was strange that at this moment she should think about Eric, and unconsciously her fingers sought the place where his ring had been. She had taken it off while handling the files and forgotten to replace it.

Grant noticed her action and his face changed abruptly, darkening with sudden suspicion. 'Where's your ring?' and when she did not answer, 'Does it mean your engagement is over, that you intend telling Bassett-Brown when you get back that it's all off? I can't believe you've at last come to your senses.'

His condemning tone shattered Cathy's warmth and she struggled up, instantly ashamed that she had been lying there, openly inviting him. 'I was afraid of losing it,' she said tightly.

'But not of losing Eric?' came the scathing reply.

She did not know what to say. She was not sure at this moment precisely what her feelings for Eric were. She knew that it was impossible to love two men at the same time and in the same way.

She looked at Grant and realised suddenly that no matter what happened she would never marry Eric. He paled into insignificance beside this strong virile man who could excite her without even knowing it.

At one time she had thought that her feelings for

Grant were purely physical. He attracted her sexually and her body had ached to be owned by him. But during the days they had worked together it had grown into something more.

She had originally wanted only to be his lover, but now she wanted to be his friend, his companion, she wanted to spend all her days and all her nights with him for the rest of her life, to share his sorrows and his joys, his ups and his downs, to bear his children and share in their pleasure.

It was true love that she felt. The fatalistic part about it was that there was no way he would ever return her feelings. Even a few minutes ago when he had taken her into his arms and looked at her with desire, she had known that his attraction was purely physical, as had been hers in the beginning.

He was a perfectly healthy male animal who wanted a woman, and she had been ready and willing. Had it not been for the intervention of Eric he might very well have taken her—and she would have shown no resistance.

'I didn't encourage you,' she said hotly.

His eyes narrowed. 'But it was what you wanted all the same, there's no denying that. You were as ready to receive me as I was——' He stopped abruptly and without another word crossed to the drinks cupboard and poured himself a whisky. He downed it in one swallow and refilled the glass before coming over to where she still stood.

Cathy felt tears prick the back of her eyes at his harsh words. She had been tempted to run out of the room while he was occupied with the bottle, but had seen this as an admission of guilt, and she had done nothing of which she could feel guilty. She had reacted as would any other girl when a man as attractive as Grant attempted to make love.

'I'd like a drink too,' she said, eyeing his glass.

'Then get yourself one,' he snapped.

She was glad of the excuse to move away and poured herself a Napoleon Brandy. Normally she took her drink diluted, but tonight she felt the need for something stronger.

'What do you suggest we do now?' asked Grant roughly. 'I'd planned on this being a pleasant evening, now I damn well wish I'd gone out.'

'There's still time, if that's what you want,' she replied tersely. 'I'm beginning to wish you had gone. Life's certainly a lot more peaceful when you're not around.'

'I could say the same about you,' he remarked acidly. 'What a fool I was to agree to your coming here! I might have known things wouldn't go smoothly.'

'They would if you'd let them.' Cathy's eyes challenged his. 'If you'd let me help, let me take part. I have a feeling we could work very well together.'

'You have?' He sounded condescending. 'I'm sorry to disillusion you, young lady, but a woman of your type is the last person I would choose as a partner, if that's the sort of relationship you're thinking about.'

'I don't know what you mean by my type,' said Cathy.

'I think you do,' he returned. 'You've done nothing but flaunt yourself at me ever since we met, and I'm still not entirely convinced that that first meeting was pure coincidence. It's happened too often in the past for me not to recognise the procedure.'

She shrugged her slim shoulders. 'Suit yourself, but I'm not in the habit of telling lies.'

'What are you going to tell Eric when you get back?' he asked abruptly. 'Perhaps I should have made love to you.' A sinister smile curved his lips. 'I wonder what he'd have said to that, or do you reckon he wouldn't have cared, so long as you managed to persuade me to sell? When are you going to put the pressure on, dear little lady? You've managed to find your way into my home, what's your next move?'

Cathy stared at him hostilely. 'You know damn well that I don't want your island, or anything connected with you!'

His lips curled derisively. 'You still believe that Eric was going to buy it for you? My God, you're more naïve than I thought! He wants it for himself, can't you see that? He'd drop you like a red-hot brick if you managed to clinch the deal. What's the matter, don't you care enough for him to do it? Doesn't even the thought that he might offer you a handsome settlement tempt you to try and persuade me to sell?'

His taunting angered Cathy, but she was determined not to lose her temper. 'The day I try and get round you for anything, *Mr* Howard, will be the day I'm certified insane!'

He took her glass and placed it upon the mantelshelf beside his own, then holding her by the shoulders drew her towards him. Her heart fluttered like the wings of a caged bird. She wondered what was coming next.

'Don't you find the challenge exciting?' he demanded. 'Wouldn't it give you a sense of power if you thought you could twist me round your little finger? Go on, let me see how you work, flutter those long lashes, part those inviting lips, rub your delicious body next to mine. You were ready and willing a few moments ago—what happened? Did you chicken out, or did thoughts of Eric prevent you? Perhaps your conscience pricked you?'

Cathy shook her head dumbly. Grant in this mood frightened her. He was angry, goading her into—into what? She knew that if he did not release her soon she would be unable to control the wild feelings that were filling her body. His virility reached out to her like a magnet, her breathing grew ragged and she stared up at him with wide blue eyes.

'You're despicable!' she managed to jerk. 'I'm not the type of woman who uses men to further her own ends. If Eric wants the island he can do his own dirty work!'

Grant laughed softly. 'You almost make me believe you did come over here with the mistaken impression that Eric was going to purchase the island for you, but I know too much about women to know how limpid blue eyes can beguile and appeal, hiding the true depth of their feelings.' A harsh light came into his eyes as though he was remembering something that was painful to him.

'It's the truth,' she cried. 'What do I have to do to make you believe it?'

'You could try being yourself,' he suggested coolly. 'One minute you're the cool efficient secretary, the sort of person I wouldn't mind taking out knowing that the evening wouldn't get out of hand, the next you're the silky seductress giving me the come-hither without so much as batting an eyelid, then crying wolf the moment I attempt to take advantage.'

How could she say that it was Grant himself who made her feel like this, that she had never acted this way in front of any other man, not even Eric? It became impossible to disguise her feelings; Grant made a wanton woman of her and there was nothing she could do about it.

His fingers tightened when she did not answer, digging painfully into the thin flesh of her shoulders. She raised her hands and pushed against him, but to no avail. He laughed and his face drew closer. Again she felt the pressure of his lips on hers, but there was no tenderness. It was meant as a punishment, was harsh and brutal, pressing her lips back against her teeth. He explored her soft moistness with savage intensity and she knew that he must be aware of her shivers of delight.

She felt as though all the stuffing had been taken out of her and that when he let her go she would fall into a crumpled heap on the floor. Her arms now instead of pushing against him were behind his back and even though she knew his kisses were a mockery she could not stop herself from responding. This man drove away all sense of shame and she was prepared to give herself up in total abandonment.

When his lips lifted for a fraction of a second she cried, 'Oh, Grant!' and it was a cry from her heart.

'Oh, Grant what?' he mocked drily, golden eyes blazing down into her face.

Cathy realised that he was not as unmoved as he made out, and she attempted to pull his head down again towards hers.

He pushed her away forcefully and she fell back against a chair, losing her balance and crashing to the floor. She expected an immediate apology, thought he would drop to his knees and pick her up, but no, for the few seconds that she lay there he gazed down dispassionately.

'You've got no more than you deserve,' he rasped

harshly. 'I can't stand women who throw themselves at me.'

'I didn't!' cried Cathy. 'I didn't, it was you—you who——'

He stopped her with an imperious wave of his hand. 'I did nothing that any full-blooded male wouldn't do when he has it handed to him on a plate. You're very attractive, Cleopatra, I'll hand you that, but even so it doesn't mean I'm going to make love to you each time you invite me.'

'Invite you?' screamed Cathy. 'I wouldn't let you even if you tried!' She knew she ought to pull herself up, but was somehow loath to meet his eyes on their own level again.

'That's a debatable point,' he said smoothly. 'I wouldn't lay a bet on it if I were you.'

She refused to answer, slowly, very slowly, pulling herself up. She was not hurt, mainly shaken, and furious with both herself and Grant for what had happened.

Picking up her drink, she finished the brandy, spluttering over the last drop, but tossing her head scornfully as she put down the glass and walked across the room. 'Goodnight, Grant. I'm sorry I can't say thanks for a pleasant evening, but it's certainly not been boring.'

His taunting reply reached her as she opened the door. 'What's the matter, Cleopatra, the pace too great for you? Perhaps you'll have second thoughts before running to my mother again with tales that I neglect you.'

So it had been Martha! She turned and glared at him. 'I've done no such thing!'

'No?' One eyebrow lifted sceptically. 'Why then

would she tell me that I must look after you better?'

'You know your mother,' returned Cathy evenly. 'I will admit I told her you went out every evening, but I couldn't lie, could I, when she asked me? But what interpretation she put on it has nothing to do with me. I wasn't moaning, if that's what you're suggesting.'

'But you have discussed me?'

'Certainly not,' replied Cathy. 'Why should I want to do that?'

He scowled. 'Women seem to take pleasure out of such things.'

'Well, I'm sorry to inform you that it's not true. Please yourself whether you believe me, I couldn't care less. I'm going to bed now—goodnight.'

Grant didn't answer, and she closed the door with a resounding bang which gave her a great deal of satisfaction. But her legs as she climbed the stairs were heavy and by the time she reached her room tears were rolling down her cheeks.

For the first time she wished there was a bolt or key so that she could lock herself in before giving vent to the emotions which were tearing her apart. She was almost afraid to cry in case Grant heard and came to gloat over her. But the tears flowed and she buried her head in the pillow, sobbing silently until at length she became calmer.

It was clear that Grant had deliberately set out to taunt her this evening, and she must learn not to take any notice if he acted this way again. There were still more than two weeks before the ferry, she must do her best to ignore any further gibes. Perhaps there wouldn't be another repetition of tonight? Perhaps he too would realise how disastrous the two of them getting together socially could be.

It was all right while they were working, while the two of them were preoccupied with their own tasks, but when they were together with nothing to do but be aware of one another, and in Cathy's case this awareness was so vital it could not be ignored, then the trouble started.

She could only hope that Grant would suggest no more intimate evenings. If he himself stayed in then she would go out; it was as simple as that. It was the only way.

Had their little scene affected him as much as it had her, she wondered, or was he laughing, things having turned out exactly as he expected. Perhaps it was what he had planned all along?

It could be that he had intended making love to her. For all she knew he could be frustrated. She had no idea where he normally spent his evenings, whether there was another woman involved or whether he went for a lonely drink at the hotel. All she knew was that he had kept clear of her. This was the first time they had really got together—and look what had happened. It had been a complete disaster, and in a way it was all Eric's fault.

She picked up his ring from the little jug on the dressing table and slipped it back on her finger. She felt safer with that there. It was a barrier between her and Grant and even though she had every intention of giving it back to Eric when she returned to England for the time being it would never be off her finger.

She spent a restless night and was down in the study long before Grant the next morning. It was unusual for her to be first, and she wondered ironically whether the events of last night had anything to do with his lateness. But somehow she doubted it. Men like Grant were immune to such upsets. It would have passed over him like water on a duck's back. No doubt he had slept deeply and soundly, so deeply in fact that he had overslept this morning.

It was nine-thirty before he came in and Cathy was surprised to see the shadows beneath his eyes. Perhaps he hadn't slept so well after all? She was glad that he too had bad nights.

She half expected an apology, was disappointed when none was forthcoming. He sat down at his desk, ignoring her as usual, but even his typing did not seem to be going so well this morning. He had intermittent bursts when he would go at great speed, then he would rip the paper out of his machine and tear it into shreds.

When Mrs P. brought their elevenses he pounced on the coffee gratefully, but still did not speak to Cathy. She fetched her own cup and returned to her corner, sipping it slowly, studying the back of his head.

As though aware of her scrutiny Grant swivelled and looked at her coldly, his eyes resting for a second on the diamond ring. 'Is anything wrong? Was there something you wanted?'

She shook her head. 'Not really. I was thinking how tired you looked when you walked in.'

'I could say the same about you,' he returned curtly. 'Your face is far from a picture of health. Didn't you sleep?'

'Not much,' she admitted.

'Because of what happened last night?'

'Oh, no,' she said quickly—too quickly, for one eyebrow rose in disbelief.

'Then why couldn't you sleep? A young girl like you should have no trouble.'

She could not tell him the truth, so she said, 'It

happens sometimes. How about you, why couldn't you sleep?'

It was a direct question and she did not expect an answer. 'Who's saying I couldn't?' he encountered hastily.

'Are you having trouble with your writing?'

That made him even more angry than before. He finished his coffee and stood up. 'Take the rest of the day off. I'm going out.'

This was so unlike Grant that she stared. He lived for his work, never once except on that first meeting had she known him not put in a full day. And Samora was so small, where was there for him to go? But she knew better than to question him, merely watching sadly as he left the room.

For a while she continued her work. She had almost come to the end of the files and would have liked to finish it, presenting Grant with his brand new system first thing in the morning, but somehow now that he had gone she had no heart in it.

She wondered whether he had forgotten his insistence that he was going to move her out of his study. It had not occurred to her again, she had to admit, until this moment, but now she began to think that it might not be a bad idea. Things between them were getting worse instead of better.

Mrs Prim came into the office at lunchtime announcing coldly that she had left a salad but was now going as Mr Howard had given her the rest of the day off.

Left alone in the house, Cathy felt even more disinclined to work. She wandered about the room and found herself drawn towards Grant's desk. Almost without realising it she sat down and began to read. The story was tragic.

It began with a young and beautiful wife very much in love with her husband, but when a baby arrived at the end of their first year of marriage she accused her husband of doing it deliberately to tie her to the house. It caused a rift between them and it was sad to see them slowly drifting apart.

When at last the husband could stand it no longer and decided to leave, taking his son with him, his wife fought against it. Although she didn't want the child she didn't want him to have him either. She kidnapped him back from the father and obtained legal custody.

He loved his son very dearly and was heartbroken, spending much time trying to persuade his wife to give up the child or reconcile herself to the fact that he belonged to them both. If she would only forget the idea that the child was tying her down to the house they could live together again. He still loved her, actually humiliated himself in front of her, but she would not agree; she kept the child, while admitting that she did not love him but would nevertheless go to any lengths to keep him away from her husband.

By the time Cathy had finished reading she felt as though she had witnessed the scenes, so vividly were they written. It was like a picture playing out on a screen before her eyes, and she wanted to know how the story ended. She wondered if she ever would, whether Grant would finish the book before she left and if she would get the chance to read the final chapters.

She hoped it had a happy ending; she did not like books that were sad. So far this one had done nothing but tear at her heartstrings and real tears slid down her cheeks. Maybe one day, when the book was published, she would read it.

Unable to face the thought of eating alone, she decided to pay Grant's parents another visit. It had been a few days since she had seen them and they were more than pleased when she appeared on their doorstep.

Martha soon had the kettle on and a cup of tea ready. 'We've been wondering how you're getting on, haven't we, Jonathan?'

Her husband nodded.

'Grant was here the other day,' she continued. 'Gave him a piece of my mind, I did. I hope it worked. Has he been treating you any better?'

Cathy shook her head wryly. 'I knew you'd said something. He stopped in last night, we had dinner together.'

'Oh, I am glad,' said his mother happily. 'You're just what my son needs, someone to take his mind off matters. He shuts himself away for far too long.'

'I'm afraid it didn't work out,' said Cathy. There was no point in lying, telling Martha that they had had a lovely evening when Grant could very well tell her a completely different tale the next time he saw them.

'Why ever not?' questioned the older woman, suddenly concerned. 'He didn't try to make a pass at you?'

She knew her son, thought Cathy with amusement. 'Nothing like that,' she lied. 'We just can't see eye to eye, that's all. We argued almost the entire evening.'

'Do you argue all day besides?' asked Jonathan.

'Oh no, we don't speak,' replied Cathy.

The two older people's eyes opened wide and they looked at each other in bewilderment. 'That doesn't sound like Grant,' said his father.

'He worries me,' added Martha. 'I thought when you came he might snap out of his lethargy. He has much on his mind, you know.'

'I know he's a busy man,' said Cathy. 'His books must take their toll. I've heard people say how very exhausting writing can be, and then there's his research.'

'Mmm,' nodded Martha, 'it's more than that, and Grant wouldn't thank me for going into detail, but—treat him gently, Cathy, he's been through a rough time.'

Cathy supposed it had something to do with his wife. A divorce, no doubt. She wondered what had happened to the child in this case. No doubt they had come to some amicable agreement. There was no way that Grant would be able to cope with a child in the house while he was writing. In their case it was far, far better for the mother to have him, not like the hard woman in the story who had held on to the child out of spite.

She suddenly realised that Martha was talking to her. 'I'm sorry,' she said. 'I was miles away.'

'Thinking about your boy-friend, I expect,' said Martha. 'You must be missing him.'

Cathy grabbed at this excuse. 'I expect he's wondering why I didn't get back as planned.'

'It's not your fault,' said Martha practically. 'I should think he'll realise that. Don't worry too much.'

Their conversation changed to everyday topics after that and soon Cathy declared it was time to go. Since the evening Grant had shouted at her for returning late she had made a point of always getting in early. Living with a person, as she did Grant, she felt it imperative to try and keep the peace, not that it always worked. Grant was a man of many moods and she never quite knew where she stood with him.

Shortly after dinner therefore she was making her

way back up the hill when a shout behind made her turn. It was Grant. She paused and waited for him to catch her up. He seemed to have forgotten his ill humour. 'Where have you been?' he asked.

'To see your parents,' she replied cautiously.

'Oh,' he said, and his smile faded. 'How are they?'

He's wondering whether I've told them about last night, she thought. 'They're fine. What have you been doing?' She half expected him to tell her to mind her own business and was surprised when he said:

'I've been walking—and thinking.' But that was as far as he went.

She presumed he had been thinking about his book as he had clearly been having difficulty with it this morning. She hoped he had got it sorted out.

In the house she asked whether he would like her to cook him some dinner.

'A sandwich will do,' he replied curtly. 'I should hate to put you to any trouble.'

Cathy tossed her head indignantly, about to make a heated reply, but he marched straight into his study and she had the feeling that it wouldn't matter to him whether he ate or not. But it mattered to her, and she made him an omelette filled with cheese and ham, and cut a slice of fruit pie cooked by his housekeeper that morning.

She loaded them on to a tray and took it into his study. He was sitting at his desk, staring into space, and Cathy had to call his name twice before he realised she was there.

He looked up and frowned, pulling himself back to the present with a jerk. She put the tray on his desk and said quietly, 'There you are, Grant, eat that. It will do you good.'

'Why the hell don't you stop fussing?' he demanded angrily.

'And why the hell don't you stop behaving like a grumpy bear?' she returned with equal ferocity. It annoyed her that whatever she did he showed no appreciation. 'You've got to eat and you gave Mrs P. the day off, so you'll have to make do with this.'

She stormed out again before he could speak and went up to her room. She could not see where the end of all this lay. Grant had changed so dramatically since that first day when he had invited her to stay for dinner. It had looked like being the beginning of a new and wonderful friendship. What had gone wrong? she wondered. Admittedly he had a wife somewhere in the background, or an ex-wife, whatever the case might be—no one wanted to tell her. And she had Eric—nevertheless there was a thin line that drew her and Grant together and she was quite sure that he must feel it as well as she.

It was beginning to mean less and less to her that he was married. It was apparent he did not see his wife, that there was no communication between them, so why should it bother her?

Divorce was so commonplace that even if he hadn't already divorced his wife it would be a simple matter. Perhaps he was afraid to fall in love again, perhaps he was keeping a tight rein on his feelings? If that was the case, thought Cathy, maybe she ought to persuade him otherwise. Perhaps she could subtly make him more aware of her, make him forget the harsh thoughts he evidently harboured.

As soon as her decision was made Cathy went back down to his study. She was pleased to see that he was eating, but even so he frowned at the interruption. 'What do you want?' he demanded heavily.

'I thought I'd join you,' she said brightly, pouring coffee into the extra cup she had put on the tray.

His frown deepened, but he didn't tell her to go, and she saw this as a good sign. She pulled up a chair and sat down, endeavouring to keep a pleasant smile on her face, difficult when he was so obviously opposed to her presence.

'Do you intend working all evening?' she ventured after a while. 'I thought we might listen to some music.'

He looked at her suspiciously. 'Now what's your game? Are we playing the seductress again? I wondered how long it would be before we got back to that. Feeling frustrated, are you? Like all women you can't do without a man for too long. Perhaps we should send for Eric? He might be willing to oblige.'

Cathy listened aghast to his sneering accusations, and stood up, feeling more insulted than she ever had in her life. 'I hate you, Grant!' she spat furiously. 'Who the devil do you think you are, God's gift to women? I'm not offering myself to you, if that's what you think. I merely thought that a little relaxation was what you needed. I'm concerned about your health, nothing more.'

'And why should you bother yourself about me?' he snorted derisively. 'My mother been at you again? Saying how her little boy works too hard.' His lip curled. 'Tell her to go to hell the next time she starts talking about me. I don't need her concern and I don't need yours. You're here to do a job, nothing more. There are no perks attached.'

Cathy didn't know whether to burst into tears or lash out. He made her absolutely furious with his illogical insinuations!

But as she had no wish to break down in front of him, and as she did not think she would get very far if she tried to hit him, she did the next best thing. With one swift movement she lifted the edge of the tray and tipped the contents on his lap. Then without waiting his reaction she fled from the room.

Not until she had flung herself down on to the bed did she allow the tears to flow, but she had been there for no more than a few seconds when she heard him bounding up the stairs.

Her door was thrust savagely open and although she did not turn she knew he stood over her, could imagine his thunderous expression. When one heavy hand caught her shoulder and spun her round she blinked back the tears and stared hostilely up into his face.

The next second she was caught a stinging blow across the cheek. She had not expected that and her eyes widened in pain and anger. She could only see a blurred image through her tears, but sufficient to note that Grant too was furiously angry. She began to struggle up, aware of a burning urge to strike back.

But he was more than ready for her. 'No woman does a thing like that to me and gets away with it,' he grated, and pinning her arms to the bed he sat astride her legs so that there was no way she could move. His eyes were two narrow slits, their tawny depths barely discernible. His nostrils flared and a pulse jerked in his jaw.

Cathy stiffened and glared belligerently, wondering what he was going to do next, and wondering what had happened to her tongue that she could not answer him back as he deserved.

She was not sorry for what she had done, but she could equally understand Grant's reaction. There was no way that he would let a woman get the better of him.

'A woman spurned,' he spat into her face, 'is that it? Is that why you did it? Were you angry with me because I refused to respond to your pathetic advances?'

She declined to answer, looking stubbornly up into his face. Her tears had stopped. She was as angry as he, tensing herself, waiting for whatever punishment he thought fit to mete out. Her cheek was burning where he had slapped her and at that precise moment she felt no love for him, merely hatred that he should treat her so despicably.

'You certainly have a high opinion of yourself, if you think that's what I was trying to do,' she said at length, when it became clear he was still waiting for her reply.

His eyes widened disbelievingly. 'For what other reason would you wish to please me? No woman does anything without selfish motives.'

'Then all I can say,' returned Cathy tightly, 'is that you've mixed with the wrong type of woman. My thoughts were for you alone. You work too hard, and that's all there is to it.'

He did not believe her, no doubt assuming it was still a ploy she was using to attract him towards her. She felt humiliated that she should have her good intentions thrown back into her face, and twisting her head sharply bit into his arm, not stopping until she felt the taste of his blood on her lips.

With a yell he let her go. 'You little bitch!' he cried

savagely, and the next moment she felt his full weight on her body. 'You're asking for it all right,' he ground, his face looming nearer.

She was determined that this time he should not kiss her and she flung her head to one side, thrashing and writhing, kicking and twisting, struggling with all her might. 'You dare kiss me,' she yelled angrily, 'and I'll bite your lips as well. You'll wish you'd never started this!'

He paused momentarily, eyes narrowed. 'I believe you would—but let's try it and find out, shall we? Let's see exactly whether you're brave enough, or woman enough, to carry out your threats.'

She expected another of his brutally punishing kisses, anticipated him pressing his lips so hard against her mouth that she would be unable to bite him. Instead his kisses were infinitely gentle, insiduously encroaching into her senses until she had no more desire to hurt him.

The maddening part was that Grant had been confident this would happen, was probably congratulating himself on his victory—and there was nothing she could do about it! Yet again she was under his spell.

His kisses were like nectar trickling down her throat, sweet and tantalising so that she craved for more. For a few long seconds she allowed herself to revel in the luxury of his caress, returning his kiss, feeling her body melt into his.

But she knew that if she did not call a halt soon it would be too late. He was so angry there would be no stopping him, yet it was a cold calculated anger. He knew exactly what he was doing, had planned it in such a way that she would never actually be able to say that he had raped her.

Tears squeezed from her eyes again, rolling down her cheeks, mingled with his kiss. He gave an exclamation of disgust and let her go. 'Feeling sorry for yourself?' he demanded, standing over the bed. 'What's happened to your fight?'

When she made no response he continued, 'You're like most women, all talk. Despite your protestations that it was not me you wanted I saw no sign of resistance, only a first abortive attempt that amounted to nothing. You're as ready and willing as the next to receive any man.'

Cathy did not try to deny this. She saw no point. If that was what he wanted to think, then let him. But it was not every man that she wanted: it was him, and him alone. She could not even face the thought of Eric making love to her, the idea of him kissing her these days was repugnant.

Grant had done this. He had made the thought of all other men distasteful. She loved only him and would do so for the rest of her life, though it was doubtful he would ever find out. He was so busy condemning her, trying to make out she was like all the other girls he had met, who were after him purely for the sake of sex alone, that he could not see her true feelings.

'Will you please go?' she asked tremulously, and the sneer on his face hurt more than his rejection. She struggled to keep back the threatening flood of tears, knowing that to break down completely in front of him would be the final humiliation. He was confident that it was all an act put on for his benefit. She could not get him any other way, so why not try this one?

'I ought to thrash you,' he declared wildly.

'For what?' she demanded. 'All I've done is become

an unwanted guest in your house, and it was through no fault of my own. I've not asked for any of this.'

'You've not?' he queried passionately. 'You could have fooled me. You're no different from any other girl I've come across.'

'Does that include your wife?' asked Cathy tightly before she could stop herself.

Grant blanched, his face tightening. 'What do you know about her? Who's been talking?'

She knew that he was insinuating that his mother had been interfering. 'Martha's said nothing,' she returned bitterly. 'I saw from one of your books that you had a wife and child. I drew my own conclusions when I never heard you mention them.'

'And may I be permitted to ask what they are?'

She shook her head. 'I have no wish to intrude into your private affairs. What I do object to is you classing me the same as everyone else.'

He stared at her for a few long seconds and all her love welled up. There was a pained look on his face and she wanted to go to him, to smooth the creases from his brow, tell him that whatever had happened in the past it did not matter, *she* would make him happy.

But she could hardly say this to a man who did not love her, who wanted nothing more than to get her out of the house; who—if he did kiss her—only did it as a form of punishment, or because there was no other girl available when he felt the need of physical fulfilment.

His cold hard eyes penetrated into her face. 'I wish to hell you'd never come here!'

Her hurt blue eyes looked back. 'And I wish to God I never had!'

CHAPTER SIX

CATHY felt apprehensive about going down to Grant's study. It was the first morning she had felt like this. Every other time she had been eager to start, but today because of her scene with Grant she felt on edge, unknowing what to expect. For all she knew he might throw her out, declare he did not want her to work with him ever again.

Last night he had stormed out of her bedroom. Occasionally she had heard his typewriter, more often than not there was silence. Once she had crept downstairs and had seen a thin line of light beneath his door, but she had not dared intrude.

She herself had slept only fitfully and now felt desperately tired, but she knew she would have to force herself to pretend that nothing had happened, or it would make the atmosphere between them even more unbearable.

Skipping breakfast, she went straight to Grant's study, bracing her shoulders before entering. He gave her a long hard look and then turned back to his typing. Cathy crossed to her desk. At least he wasn't going to throw her out, that was something.

They worked steadily throughout the morning, only stopping when Mrs Prim brought in their coffee. Even then Grant did not speak, and Cathy herself made no attempt at conversation.

At lunchtime she went into the dining room and ate a solitary lunch. Grant ignored her when she asked whether he was coming and when she returned a half hour later he was still typing away as though his life depended on it. His mental block of yesterday had certainly gone. She had never seen him work quite so hard, driving himself desperately, and she gathered it would not be long before his book was finished. She hoped there would be an opportunity for her to read through these final chapters.

By mid-afternoon she had finished, both the filing and the index were complete. She sat for a while staring out of the window at the beautiful tropical flowers and the blue Indian Ocean.

For some unknown reason she felt the need to escape, wanted to get away from Grant and his overpowering resentment towards her. She dared to interrupt him. 'I've finished the files, Grant. May I have the rest of the day off? I feel like a swim.'

He looked at her doubtfully, almost as though he hadn't heard a word she said, then he nodded. She paused a moment, expecting something more, but when he returned again to his typing she shrugged and left the room.

It did not take her long to put on her bikini and a short towelling dress and make her way down the hill to the beach. The water was warm and inviting and she swam vigorously for several minutes before turning on her back and floating lazily.

After a while she returned to the shore and she was lying on the sand, almost asleep, when she heard a boat approaching.

She shot up and shaded her eyes, excitement coursing through her veins. Perhaps she could beg a lift back to Mahé? Perhaps the end of her torment would be over sooner than she thought.

As the boat came nearer she could see that it was the same one that had brought her out to Samora—he had turned up after all! She waved ecstatically and went down to the wooden pier.

To her amazement it was not the boatman who climbed out—but Eric!

Some of her happiness faded, even though she knew it shouldn't have—he was her fiancé, after all. He came swiftly towards her and gathered her into his arms. 'Cathy, I was so worried! You can't imagine my relief when I discovered that Philippe had simply been having trouble with his boat. I thought something had happened to you.'

When she remained unresponsive in his arms he held her away and looked enquiringly down into her face. 'What's the matter, aren't you pleased to see me?'

He was exactly as she remembered him, tall, good-looking, self-assured; the only difference was in her own attitude. He no longer had the power to cause her heart to skip a beat; she could look at him and feel nothing at all.

She gave a little laugh that was not entirely convincing. 'I was upset,' she said, 'when the boat didn't come. I didn't know what I was going to do.'

'Not half so worried as me,' said Eric strongly. 'That's why I'm here.'

'And why didn't he come?' she asked crossly, glancing back at the boat and the man who stood on the deck. 'If he'd had trouble surely he could have hired another boat, not left me stranded here with not so much as a word to say what was wrong? How do you think I felt?'

It disturbed her, Eric being here. Although she had wanted nothing more than to get away from Samora, to leave behind the man with whom she had fallen unwillingly into love, she had not wanted Eric here, could not bear the thought of the two men meeting again.

'All's well that ends well,' he said matter-of-factly. 'Surely you've enjoyed yourself?'

'It's a beautiful island,' admitted Cathy. 'You couldn't have chosen anything better for a wedding present. It's absolutely marvellous!'

Had she not been watching him closely she would not have seen the faint altering of his expression. For a few seconds he looked taken aback, but he pulled himself together quickly and smiled down into his fiancée's face. 'Nothing but the best is good enough for you, my darling.'

She had never realised before what a good actor he was. Even now she had difficulty in believing that he was not sincere. Had it not been for Grant's warning she would never have guessed that Eric did not fully intend buying her this island.

She wondered what he would say when he discovered that she had met Grant and that he had told her he had no intention of selling? Would he hide his feelings so well then?

'Come on,' he said, draping an arm about her shoulders. 'Let's go to the hotel and you can tell me all that's been happening.'

'I'm not at the hotel any longer,' she said hesitantly. 'They're full. They had no room for me after my two days were up.'

'Then where are you staying?' he queried, anxiously she thought.

'I've got a room in a private house. I was fortunate enough to find someone willing to put me up. When the boat didn't come I realised I'd be stuck here for another three weeks, until the next ferry at least. I was worried about letting you know, but there was nothing I could do about it. You never warned me how isolated it was.'

'That's why I like it,' he said brusquely. 'Where's this place you're staying? Will they have room for me? I'd planned on stopping a day or two since I've gone to all the trouble of getting here.'

Trouble, thought Cathy wryly. Was that what he considered checking on her safety to be? But she kept her thoughts to herself for the moment, saying cautiously, 'It's not far,' wondering whether to break the news now or let him find out for himself that she was living with, according to Grant, his arch-enemy.

But as she led the way up the hill he looked at her in surprise. 'You're not staying with Grant Howard, by any chance?'

She nodded. 'He was the only person with enough room. Have you any objections?'

He looked uneasy. 'None at all. Did he tell you that we knew each other?'

'Oh, yes,' she replied easily. 'I understand you were at Oxford together. How nice for you. You'll be able to reminisce about old times.'

But Eric did not look too happy about the situation and was silent. She realised he wanted to ask her what had transpired between her and Grant Howard but had difficulty in framing his question without appearing too concerned. And she herself did not give him much chance, chatting brightly about what a beautiful place Samora was and how indebted she was to him for wanting to buy it her.

It gave her great pleasure, she realised surprisingly,

to put Eric into this uncomfortable position. During the few days they had been apart she had grown detached from him, Grant had made her realise that he was not the loving man she had once thought, and now that she had seen his reaction for herself it confirmed that Grant had been speaking the truth.

She had never wanted to doubt Grant, but there had always been that niggling thought at the back of her mind that he could be wrong. Amazingly she was glad that he wasn't.

Grant would never love her, she knew, but at least he had done her the favour of telling her about Eric before she herself found out the hard way. She wondered whether to give him back his ring now before it all came to a head, or allow things to take their course and see what happened when he realised that she had found him out for what he really was.

By this time they had reached the house. She walked inside and went straight to Grant's study. Eric followed at an appreciable distance. Cathy pushed open the door, for once not caring that she interrupted him.

'You have another visitor, Grant,' she said abruptly. 'Do you think you'll be able to put him up for a couple of nights?'

Grant whirled and looked over her shoulder, his brow darkening when he saw Eric enter the room. 'So we meet again,' he said tightly. 'Come to collect your fiancée, have you? I'm sorry to tell you she's been unable to pull off the deal.'

'You told her?' asked Eric at once, looking anxiously from Grant to Cathy.

'Of course,' said Grant blithely. 'Wasn't that why you sent her—to try and *persuade* me to sell after you'd failed?'

Eric looked distinctly uneasy, and Cathy smiled across at him sweetly. 'Yes, Grant did tell me that you'd tried for years to get him to sell. Why didn't you tell me? I felt a bit of a fool when I told him I'd come here to view the island because you were going to buy it for me as a wedding present. He has no intention of selling, didn't you know that?'

Before Eric could answer Grant said derisively, 'You thought she'd be able to clinch the deal for you. You chose her well, Bassett-Brown, I'll grant you that, but it still didn't work.'

'I did no such thing,' said Eric swiftly. 'I never intended that Cathy should meet you, I merely wanted her to see the island. I knew that in good time you'd sell.'

'Like hell you did,' snapped Grant. 'You knew damn well I'd never sell to you, not under any circumstances. Not even with your charming fiancée's aid.' He looked at Cathy suggestively as he spoke and Eric gave an angry snarl of suspicion.

'What have you two been up to? Grant, if you've been——'

Before he could put his suspicions into words Grant said swiftly, 'If you're foolish enough to let your pretty friend out of your sight, Bassett-Brown, then you must accept the consequences.'

Eric rounded hotly on Cathy. 'If you've been two-timing me, Cathy, then you can count our engagement finished here and now!'

'What did I tell you?' drawled Grant, his eyes twinkling as he looked across at her. 'Entirely predictable.'

'What are you talking about?' demanded Eric, his face suffused with dark angry colour.

Cathy had never seen him angry before, he had always been charming towards her. It made her realise that it had all been a front, that he was only courteous when everything was going his way. When things went wrong, as now for instance, he was far from polite.

'If that's the way you feel,' she protested heatedly, 'then you can have your ring!' She wrenched it from her finger and threw it across the room. 'Although I can assure you that there's nothing going on between Grant and me.'

He looked as though he regretted his hasty words and picking up the ring walked slowly towards her. 'In that case, Cathy,' he said, quite humbly she thought, 'perhaps I was a bit hasty.' He lifted her hand and attempted to replace the ring, but Cathy snatched her hand away.

'I think, Eric, there are things we should discuss in private.'

Grant, looking distinctly amused, shrugged his broad shoulders. 'Feel free,' he said, and walked out of the study, closing the door with exaggerated care behind him.

Once they were alone Eric attempted to pull Cathy into his arms, his eager lips seeking hers. But she was repulsed by his touch, pushing against him with all her strength, and he let her go, a hurt expression on his face.

'You've changed,' he said. 'Are you quite sure there's nothing happened between you and him? I know what he's like. He can't be trusted where women are concerned, especially dark-haired beauties like you.'

Is that why you chose me? she wanted to ask. Is that why you sent me to do your dirty work? Her eyes were pained. 'I'm not so sure you're not the one who can't be trusted.'

He looked surprised. 'What do you mean?' and he sat down on Grant's chair, swivelling to face her.

'You got me out here under false pretences. Grant told me you've been after Samora for years and know quite well that he has no intention of selling.'

'It's true,' admitted Eric. 'But I still thought I might eventually be able to persuade him to change his mind. That's why I wanted you to see it first. There was no point in my going on with it if you didn't like the island.'

Cathy didn't believe him and her eyes narrowed as she looked into his handsome face. He was certainly better looking than Grant, with his waving brown hair always perfectly in place, his fresh complexion and clear grey eyes, though for the life of her she could not see why she had allowed herself to be tricked into thinking that she loved him, and that he loved her.

Grant had said that he used people and she was quite willing to believe this. He had used her. 'Are you trying to tell me,' she probed, 'that it had never crossed your mind that I might be able to persuade Grant to sell where you'd failed?'

'The thought never occurred to me,' he returned evenly, but Cathy had the feeling he was not telling the truth. 'What's he been saying to you? He's been getting at you behind my back, hasn't he? He's been turning you against me. I sensed something different about you the moment I landed.'

Cathy shrugged. 'He told me a few things he thought I ought to know.'

'And you believed him?'

'Not at first, but after a while when I got thinking about it I realised that there could be some truth in what he said. And your reaction when you discovered I'd met Grant gave you away. It is true, everything he said. You used me, Eric. You really thought I would be able to influence him to sell. I'm sorry to say you were wrong. In fact I would say he's even more determined than ever to keep the island.'

Eric swore violently beneath his breath. 'Trust a woman to muck things up!'

'I did no such thing,' she defended hotly. 'I had no idea when I came out here that I was supposed to be your ambassador, that I was supposed to treat Grant with the utmost care, twist him round my little finger. There's no chance of that, I'll tell you now. We get on together like two fighting cocks. Grant doesn't like me, he thinks that I was in on this right from the start, even though I've told him repeatedly that I wasn't.'

'You sound bothered,' said Eric. 'Are you?'

His blunt question took her by surprise and a glimpse of Cathy's hurt showed in her eyes before she was able to disguise it.

'He's not your type,' continued Eric.

'Neither are you,' she countered hotly. 'I've realised that. It was all a mistake, getting engaged. I fell for your good looks and your money. I've grown up since coming here. It's all over, Eric, though I suspect it would have been anyway once you discovered I was unable to succeed in the task you'd set me.'

This time he did not deny it, and crossing over to her own desk Cathy sat down. The trauma of the last few minutes had taken its toll and she felt weak, almost faint, and she wished Eric would go and leave her in peace. Not that there would ever be any peace. Her world had been turned upside down and she doubted whether she would see anything in quite the same perspective again.

She closed her eyes and as though in answer to her prayers the next time she looked up Eric had gone. She drew a deep breath and wondered what was going to happen next. Eric had said he intended staying for a few days; would he, now that things were over between them, especially since Grant was so dogmatic about refusing to sell?

There was no reason any more for him to stay, except—she suddenly remembered—there was no boat! Until his friend came back he had no choice—but when he did go she would ask him to take her with them. The next few days would be uncomfortable, she knew that, and there was nothing she could do about it.

For several long minutes she remained in the study and then Grant returned. He looked at her closely. 'So your engagement is finally off. Sorry I had to be in on the scene.'

Cathy shrugged. 'It doesn't matter. You knew about it anyway.'

'You mean it was all my fault?' His eyes held hers.

'In a way,' she admitted, 'although I suppose I would have found out eventually.'

'Are you upset?'

'As if you'd care,' she replied scathingly, 'but as a matter of fact I'm not. I've grown used to the idea during the last few days and I'm actually relieved that it's all come to a head.'

'So what are your plans now?' Grant asked.

He looked interested, but she was not so sure. 'I don't know,' she said tiredly. 'I shall go back to England with Eric, but I shan't return to his firm. I shall find myself another job, if I can.'

'You could stay on here and help me,' he said surprisingly. 'You've made a good job of those files. You're the best secretary I've ever had.'

There was nothing Cathy would have liked more, but she knew that his suggestion was impossible. She wondered why he had made it. 'No, Grant, it wouldn't work. Now I've got you sorted out, though, I'm sure you'll cope. So long as you keep your files in order you should never have any difficulty in finding anything you want.'

'My files are of minimal importance,' he said brusquely. 'There are other things I can find you to do, but I should hate to keep you here against your will.'

'I'm here until Saturday,' she said, 'when Eric's boatman comes. I hope you don't mind putting him up too?'

He shrugged. 'I don't seem to have any choice. I just hope the two of you will keep out of my way. I still have my work to do, you know.'

Cathy nodded, her eyes pained. 'I know, Grant, and I'm sorry.'

She had meant that she was sorry Eric has forced his presence on him, but he seemed to think she was saying sorry for refusing to carry on working for him.

He shrugged and sat down at his typewriter. 'Go and amuse yourself, Cathy. Let me get on with my work.'

'I'm not a child,' she returned irritably, resenting his inference. 'If there's anything I can do I will while I'm here.'

'And how about Eric?' he asked imperiously.

'What's he going to think? Does he know you've been working for me?'

She shook her head. 'It's nothing to do with him. It's none of his business any longer. He can please himself what he thinks.'

'Knowing him as well as I do,' replied Grant, 'he still won't be happy at the thought of you shut in here with me all day long. Eric can be very jealous, and even though you're no longer officially engaged he may well still resent the fact that another man is taking an interest.'

'But you're not,' returned Cathy heatedly. 'We'd only be working.'

'We know that,' replied Grant diffidently, 'but would he?'

'I suppose not, but I can't stay on here and accept free lodgings. You must let us pay.'

He smiled strangely. 'I'm sure Eric will take care of that. Now run along, there's a good girl. You've held me up quite enough.'

Cathy felt choked when she left his study, and matters were made worse when she found Eric waiting outside. He looked at her tear-filled eyes. 'What's he been saying to you?'

'Nothing much,' she replied, shaking her head.

'It doesn't look like it,' he growled. 'If I thought he'd been getting at you I'd go in there and teach him a lesson!'

Then why don't you? thought Cathy. Eric was all talk and no action, and she was despising him more by the minute. 'It beats me why you want the island anyway,' she said. 'There's nothing to do, I can't see you being happy.'

'That's precisely it,' he said. 'I have plans, big plans, Cathy. It would be an investment. Don't you realise there's only the one hotel on this island? I intend making it into a tourist's paradise. There's the whole of the other side yet to be exploited. It could make me a fortune.'

Cathy thought of Martha and Jonathan, and felt sick. 'I can't think what I ever saw in you, Eric,' she said disgustedly. 'All you ever think about is money and yourself. Your own greed will be the ruin of you one day!'

His eyes glinted mockingly. 'I don't know what you're talking about. It's what this island needs, a good shaking up. It's been going on in this same sleepy little way for years.'

'And if Grant has anything to do with it,' retorted Cathy heatedly, 'it will go on like this for a good many more. How do you think he'd be able to work if it was turned into a big holiday resort—people all over the place, spoiling his quiet?'

'You've really got it bad for him, haven't you?' sneered Eric.

'So what if I have, it's no business of yours, not any longer.'

'And it would appear that it's no business of Grant's. I don't see him returning your feelings.'

'He doesn't,' admitted Cathy sadly. 'When you leave I shall come with you and I don't suppose I shall ever see him again.' Her whole fear was emptied out into those few words.

Eric said sarcastically, 'My heart bleeds.'

She felt like scratching his eyes out, but didn't dare cause a scene in Grant's house. 'I'll go and find the housekeeper,' she said primly, 'tell her we have an extra one for dinner.' She left him standing there.

Mrs P. was far from pleased to hear about their unexpected visitor, and she demanded that Cathy look after him until she had time to show him to his room. 'I shall have to get one ready,' she said angrily, 'and there's dinner to be seen to. Why didn't someone let me know he was coming?'

'We didn't know,' said Cathy anxiously.

'He's been here before,' Mrs P. told her tersely. 'I don't like him. The last time he came I told Grant I'd never cook another meal for him again. What's he doing letting him into the house?'

Cathy said uneasily, 'He came to see me, actually. He was my fiancé—but he isn't any longer.'

'I'm glad to hear it,' said the housekeeper, and for one moment her face softened.

Cathy found Eric on the terrace, sitting on one of the wrought iron chairs beneath a red umbrella. He had stripped off his shirt and although the sun was by no means as hot as it had been during the day there was still enough warmth in it for him to feel uncomfortable, coming as he had from England's much colder climate.

Cathy could not help comparing his body with Grant's. It was pale and inclined to flabbiness, and she wondered anew what she had ever seen in him. She had been flattered by his interest, that was all, she realised sadly. She had been as stupid as a schoolgirl with her first crush. She had allowed his wealth and the fact that he had shown an interest to go to her head.

'Would you like a drink?' she asked.

'Something cool, perhaps,' he suggested easily.

She returned to the kitchen, relieved to be away from Eric. She was amazed at her sudden change of heart, unable to understand how she could transfer her affections from one man to another without compassion.

She filled a jug of water into which she placed a good handful of crushed ice and put it on a tray together with a decanter of lime and two glasses. Ignoring Mrs P.s outraged expression, she carried it out on to the terrace.

If she had to spend the next few days with Eric she realised unhappily that she would have to do her best to overcome her recent dislike of him, do her best to make his stay as pleasant as possible.

Clearly Grant would ignore them, he would shut himself away in his study, and it would be up to her to do the entertaining. At one time, before coming out to Samora and meeting Grant, there was nothing she would have liked better than to be with Eric for the greater part of each day, but now the task assumed enormous proportions and she sat down heavily on the chair, not realising that she sighed deeply.

Eric looked at her questioningly. 'I'm sorry things haven't turned out.'

'Who for?' she snapped. 'For yourself—because I didn't succeed in getting the island for you?'

He looked hurt, but she knew it was all an act.

'I'm sorry I didn't pull it off,' she said bitterly, 'but even if I had done the engagement would still be over, wouldn't it? You used me. You tried to get me to do what you yourself had failed. I'm sorry if I was a poor gullible girl taken in by your charm and good looks.'

He touched her arm. 'Cathy, you can't blame me for trying,' and he looked like a little boy hurt.

Some of her anger died. 'I would never blame anyone for trying anything, but the least you could have done was tell me. You have no idea how humiliated I've been. Grant's pretty good at doing that to people.'

At that moment the housekeeper appeared, looking coldly at Eric. 'I'll show you your room now,' she said distantly.

He rose and picking up his shirt slung it across one shoulder. 'See you later, Cathy,' he said, the woman's hostility not bothering him in the least.

Cathy remained on the terrace sipping her lime, reflecting on the events of the day. When she woke that morning she had had no idea that Eric would turn up like this. In one way she was thankful that events had been precipitated, but coming on top of last night's upset she now felt totally exhausted and wished that instead of having to spend the evening with the two men she could go to her room and fall into bed and sleep away her troubles.

She closed her eyes and for a few minutes did doze off. It was not until a gentle touch woke her that she realised she had been sitting here for longer than she intended.

Grant smiled drily down. 'It's almost time for dinner. It should prove quite a party. Think you're up to it?'

'Of course I am,' she replied, goaded by his words. He must have known that she was dreading the evening, deliberately taunting her so that she would be on her mettle and be prepared for any eventuality.

'Then you'd better run along and put on your best bib and tucker.'

He was treating her like a child again, and she lifted her chin determinedly, brushing past him without another word, but even that fleeting touch sent electric currents through her body and when she reached her room she found herself trembling.

If only Grant had been on her side then perhaps she would have had the strength to get through the evening, but with both of them against her it was going to be hard.

She chose a cool green cotton that was really intended for beach wear. It was strapless and not a dress that she would have normally chosen for such an occasion, but it was the best she could do out of her limited wardrobe—she couldn't wear the pink dress again.

When she went downstairs Grant and Eric were already in the dining room, drinks in their hands, from all outward appearances talking together as though they were old buddies, only the strained atmosphere giving away the fact that they were doing nothing more than making forced polite conversation.

Cathy fixed a smile to her lips and walked towards them. Grant poured her a drink and his fingers touched hers briefly as he handed it to her. Her eyes flickered and she knew he was aware of her reaction. He smiled briefly.

'Lucky you,' he said, and even to her ears his tone was false, 'dining with two men, or should I say lucky us, dining with such a beautiful lady?' His eyes dropped insolently to the cleavage revealed by the low-cut dress, and she felt swift colour flood her cheeks.

Eric frowned angrily and she knew he was thinking she had not told him the truth when she had said there was nothing between her and Grant.

Well, there wasn't, was there? she argued with herself. After all, Grant was only human, any man would look at a woman he was forced to dine with, especially someone in a dress as revealing as hers.

'I was just telling Eric what a good job you've made of my filing system,' said Grant cheerfully. 'He's a lucky man to have such a good secretary.'

Eric's brows rose. 'You didn't tell me you worked for Grant,' he said accusingly.

'I saw no necessity,' she replied. 'I'm doing it as a favour, in exchange for my board and lodging. I couldn't stay without paying and as I hadn't enough money on me it was the only solution.'

She lied, she knew. It had been Grant's idea that she work, in fact he had insisted upon it. Exactly why she had chosen to say this she was not sure, but for some reason she did not want to put Grant into a bad light.

'I expect you're eager to have her back,' continued Grant drily.

'I'm not going to work for him any more,' said Cathy, 'I've already told you that. Once I'm back in England I shall find myself another job.'

'You won't even work out your notice?' reproved Grant, and she knew he was deliberately trying to make things awkward.

'Not unless Eric insists?' She looked at her ex-fiancé questioningly.

He shook his head. 'I think I'd prefer if Cathy didn't come back, under the circumstances.'

Grant's lips twisted wryly. 'Because she failed in the task you set her?'

Cathy flashed him a glance. 'When are you going to believe I knew nothing about Eric wanting to buy the island?'

'I doubt I ever shall,' said Grant. 'It's one of those things, isn't it?'

Eric snapped, 'Damn you, Grant! Why are you so hateful towards Cathy? I really thought she was the type who would appeal to you.'

'Then you admit that you sent her here for a purpose?'

Eric sighed and shook his head. 'Yes and no. I did send her here hoping, I must admit, but Cathy herself knew nothing about it. I thought that if you two met accidentally you might become good friends.'

'And after that it would be a simple matter to get her to do your dirty work for you?'

'Something like that,' shrugged Eric indifferently.

'What a pity it didn't work,' sneered Grant. 'Now you've lost both Cathy and the island, or aren't you bothered about her? It wouldn't be the first girl you've chosen for your own ends alone.'

Eric looked uncomfortable.

Cathy said quickly, 'Do we really have to discuss things that have happened in the past?' She felt sorry for Eric—after all, she had once been in love with him, or thought she was, and she did not like to see him put down by this hard man. She still had some feelings for him and resented the way Grant was behaving.

Grant shrugged nonchalantly. 'If Eric's so blatant about his friendships why shouldn't we talk about them?'

Eric frowned. 'What I do is no concern of yours, Grant.'

'It is when you involve me,' replied Grant. 'By your own admittance you hoped Cathy would get to know me. If it's any consolation to her I think it was a very mean trick.'

A TASTE OF PARADISE

'It's done no harm,' said Eric indifferently.

'It hasn't got you what you wanted,' pointed out Grant.

Eric pulled a wry face. 'It doesn't mean I shall stop trying.'

The other man's eyes narrowed. 'You'd be wasting your time. Don't think I don't know why you want to buy Samora. I'm not so naïve as to think you want it purely for your own pleasure.'

Eric looked sharply at Cathy. 'What have you been saying?'

Cathy shook her head, but before she could speak Grant said, 'She's told me nothing, but I know *you*. I know exactly what sort of things run through that mind of yours. Don't forget when we were at Oxford you used to discuss the big ideas you had for the future expansion of your father's business. I'm pleased you've got on, but I certainly don't intend letting you spoil this beautiful island. There's far too much of that in the world already.'

If they were going to go on like this for the rest of the evening, thought Cathy, it was going to be hell. 'Can't you two talk about something else?' she demanded, looking sharply from one to the other.

Grant smiled, a slow lazy smile, and came across to her, resting his hand on her shoulder. A tingling awareness ran through her and she moved swiftly away. 'Does Cleopatra object to us having a friendly discussion?'

'Friendly?' she protested, ignoring Eric's startled look. 'If that's friendly goodness help me if you two ever have a real argument!'

'I agree with Cathy,' said Eric decisively. 'There's

no point in us carrying on this discussion—not at the moment.'

'Not ever,' stated Grant. He finished his drink and took Cathy's empty glass from her. 'Time we ate, don't you think?'

For reasons known only to himself Grant paid Cathy a great deal of attention during the meal. Several times she saw Eric looking at her closely and she felt distinctly uneasy. More so because she knew that Grant was doing it deliberately, that had they been alone he would have scarcely spoken to her. She wondered what devious thoughts were going through his mind.

After dinner they went into the garden room and Grant put on a record. He poured Eric a drink and then took Cathy into his arms, leading her on to the small square of floor that was free of furniture. 'You'll excuse us, Eric?' he deferred to the other man.

His movements were sensuous, his body pressed against hers, thigh touching thigh, her breast against his chest. She was intensely aware of the magnetism that flowed from him into her, and had it not been for Eric's thunderous face she would have given herself up to the pleasure of the moment.

No doubt Eric thought that this was the sort of thing they did every evening, and she wished she felt angry with Grant for deliberately giving this impression. But how could she be angry with the man she loved? Even though she knew it was all an act, that prior to Eric coming here he had shown no interest, it didn't matter. Her engagement to Eric was over so why worry what he thought?

After a few minutes in Grant's arms Cathy's emotions had reached such a pitch that she did not care whether Eric was watching or not. She lifted her head and as though he had been waiting for this moment Grant kissed her full on the lips, a passionate, consuming kiss that shook her to the core, even though she knew it meant nothing to him, that it was all a pretence for the benefit of the man who sat watching.

Eric gave a sudden snort and stood up. He crashed his glass on to the table and left the room.

Immediately Grant let her go. 'I wonder what's the matter with him?' he asked mildly.

'I think you know,' she responded. 'What was that all about? What did you hope to gain?'

'I was showing him what a silly man he was to let go such a beautiful girl as you.'

'You're not being fair on Eric,' she protested indignantly.

'Has he been fair on me?' he returned. 'By his own admittance he hoped that you and I would meet. What did he think we'd do, be platonic friends? He knows me better than that, Cathy. This is what he expected, I'm merely trying to prove him right.'

'But he wasn't right,' cried Cathy passionately, 'and you know it. Before today you scarcely bothered with me, except when it pleased you to amuse yourself. You did this deliberately to make me feel uncomfortable!'

His thick dark brows lifted mockingly. 'That was the last emotion I would guess you were feeling. You wanted me, dear Cleopatra, as much as I wanted you, whether Eric was here or not.'

'Of all the conceited, arrogant men you top the lot,' she cried coldly.

'Okay, so deny it.'

He knew she couldn't and she stared at him angrily.

'You're being unfair. You must know, a man of your expertise, what sort of a reaction you would arouse, but to do it to spite Eric is despicable.'

'And the fact that he sent you here wasn't, I suppose?' he queried testily.

She shrugged. 'I don't know about that. I'm not even sure that it's what he did.'

'Not after his own admission?'

She shook her head. 'He could have said it because he knew it was what you wanted him to say.'

Grant's eyes narrowed. 'Are you still under the impression that you're in love with him? Is that why you stick up for him?'

Cathy refused to answer. 'I'm going to find Eric. I think you ought to apologise.'

'For what?' he asked coldly.

'For behaving like this in front of him.'

He smiled insolently. 'Eric knew exactly what I was doing. I think that at last he's got the message. He's realised that sending you out here was the worst thing he could have done. I have the feeling he does care for you, a little bit, in his own peculiar way, and it's gone against the grain to see me making a fuss of you. It ought to be him, don't you think? After all, you did once promise to marry him, you must have declared your love. What do you feel for him now?'

Cathy glared angrily. 'It's no concern of yours, Grant. I'd thank you to mind your own business!'

'What if I make it my concern?' he suggested softly, insinuatingly, and reaching out he took her by the shoulders, pulling her towards him, his hands warm and firm against her skin.

She felt her heartbeats quicken, her breathing already beginning to grow ragged. She closed her eyes,

A TASTE OF PARADISE 141

not wanting to see his face. He was doing this only to torment her, not because of any feelings he might have.

He smoothed his hands about her bare back and before she realised what he was doing he had slid down the zip, allowing her dress to fall and reveal her naked breasts.

He cupped them in his hands, stroking and teasing until the nipples grew hard. He lowered his head to hers, his lips moving gently over her face, dropping kisses on to each eyelid and across her smooth cheeks, nibbling her earlobe, whispering passionately,

'Don't go back with Eric, Cleopatra. Stay here with me.'

CHAPTER SEVEN

GRANT was joking! He had to be. There was no way that he could mean what he said. Cathy looked at him, her wide blue eyes puzzled, but when she would have spoken he stopped her with a kiss and she became soft and quiescent in his arms.

After a few seconds she struggled to free herself, knowing that if he did not let her go soon she would be in danger of agreeing to his request, and although it was the very thing she wanted most, living with Grant was out of the question.

She was convinced his suggestion had something to do with Eric. In some way he wanted to get his own back on this man and he was using her in exactly the same way as he had accused her one-time fiancé.

Besides, there was his wife to consider. She still did not know whether he was divorced or not. It was not a subject she could discuss. The one and only time she had mentioned his wife he had been so angry she knew she dared not raise the subject again.

His kisses threatened to suffocate her and his hands continued their assault. I must get free, Cathy told herself frantically. Another few minutes and all will be over.

She managed to drag her lips away. 'Please let me go, Grant,' she said desperately.

Surprisingly he did. He stood back a pace, looking down at her half naked body. She pulled up her dress and awkwardly zipped it into place, Grant making no attempt to help.

'I'm waiting for your answer,' he said softly.

'You know I can't.'

'Still feeling guilty about Eric?'

She shook her head. 'There's nothing between Eric and me any more, but I still can't stay here with you. It wouldn't work.'

'Why not?' he rasped, and in sudden fury. 'Why the hell not?'

'Because,' she said patiently, 'we're incompatible. We might be sexually attracted, but that's all.'

His brow darkened. 'What makes you think I'm asking you to stay for any other reason?'

Cathy's cheeks flamed in sudden searing humiliation. What a fool she was to have thought he meant anything else other than for her to stay as his mistress! He wanted her merely to satisfy the cravings of his own body.

Physically they were compatible, but that was all. In Cathy's mind this was not enough. She loved Grant deeply and she wanted him for reasons other than sex.

'I shan't ask you again,' he said slowly, distinctly.

'My answer is still no,' she replied quietly. 'Please may I go now?'

He nodded curtly and turned his back on her. She knew that her refusal had annoyed him and could only assume that it was because he was not used to being turned down. How many women he had had here she would never know, but it stood to reason that no man as virile as Grant would lead a life of celibacy.

She wanted nothing more now than to go straight to bed, but at the top of the stairs Eric waited. He caught her arm roughly and dragged her into his room.

Cathy noticed briefly that in contrast to her own stark little bedroom this one was the height of luxury, but she spared it no more than a cursory glance, sitting down heavily on the edge of the bed. 'What do you want?' she asked curtly. 'I'm tired, and I don't think there's anything more we have to discuss.'

'On the contrary,' said Eric thickly, 'there's much to talk about. Firstly, why did you lie to me? Why did you say there was nothing between you and Grant when the evidence is there before my eyes?'

She lifted her bare shoulders and let them drop again. 'He was putting it on. It was all an act for your benefit, didn't you guess that?'

'You seemed to be enjoying it.'

'So what? He's a physically exciting man. Any girl would enjoy dancing with him.'

'Dancing, yes,' he said, 'but being made love to, that's a different thing.'

'It was all for your benefit,' she insisted. 'He stopped the moment you'd gone.'

'You expect me to believe that?' he queried testily. 'I'm not completely stupid, Cathy.'

'Anyway,' she demanded, 'wasn't that what you wanted? Wasn't it your intention to get me and Grant together so that I could use my influence to get him to sell you the island?'

'It was,' he agreed unashamedly, 'but I didn't expect you to go the whole way with him.'

'I've done no such thing!' she denied hotly.

'Oh no? The way you looked at each other it sure wasn't the first time you'd got together.'

'It's your fault if we have,' said Cathy, realising that, like Grant, he would not believe the truth if she told him. 'You sent me here, so you'll have to accept the consequences.'

'You're no concern of mine any more,' he said brusquely.

'Then why all the fuss because I've been dancing with Grant?'

'Because I didn't like the way you threw yourself at him,' he said, 'making yourself cheap.'

'I did no such thing!'

'I saw you with my own eyes.'

Some of her anger faded. 'I couldn't help myself, Eric,' she said quietly. 'I love Grant. I'm sorry it had to happen like this, but there it is.'

'And he doesn't know?' His brows lifted. 'It wouldn't do you any good if he did—he's already married. Has he told you that?'

Cathy thought he took great delight in imparting this piece of information. 'I already know,' she said pointedly.

He looked surprised. 'And it makes no difference?'

'Of course it makes a difference,' she cried, 'but it didn't stop me falling in love. That was something over which I had no control. But I do have control over whether I stay here or not. He's asked me to, but I shan't. I shall go back to England with you.'

'How noble,' he sneered, 'giving up the man you love for the sake of protocol. I wonder what he'd say if I told him you loved him?'

'Don't you dare!' she snapped, wishing now that she had said nothing. 'Besides, you never really loved me, did you, Eric? If you had you wouldn't be taking all this so calmly.'

'Clever girl, how did you guess?'

'I didn't—Grant told me. He said that it was not the first time you had done this sort of thing. I guess I made an idiot of myself.'

He shrugged. 'It was fun while it lasted. You followed the same pattern as everyone else. One day I'm going to meet a girl who'll see through me, and that will probably be the one I'll marry. Meantime it amuses me to play about.'

At that moment Cathy hated Eric. He was so blatantly offhand about the whole situation. She was glad she had found out now what he was like instead of when she got back to England full of plans and enthusiasm for Samora. It would have been doubly hard to bear then if he had told her that their engagement was over, that it had been no more than a game to him, she had served her purpose and was no longer needed.

She stood up. 'I can't see that we have anything more to discuss, Eric. It's a pity you're not going home tomorrow.'

He smiled maliciously. 'I don't know. The next few days should prove fun. I shall enjoy seeing what happens between you two. He's a very experienced man, Cathy. Be careful that he too isn't taking you for a ride.'

'As if you'd care!' she said angrily, crossing swiftly towards the door. 'Goodnight, Eric.'

'Goodnight, Cathy, pleasant dreams.'

She banged the door. It was ironical that both of them had expressed interest in seeing what happened over the next couple of days. Only she herself, the centre party, could see nothing amusing in being used as a toy to be picked up and discarded whenever they liked.

It was going to be another one of those nights, she thought as she undressed ready for bed. The two men had both succeeded in their different ways in unsettling her and she wished with all her heart that it was tomorrow the boat was coming.

Early the next morning Cathy let herself out of the house and made her way down to the beach. There was no one about and as she walked along the silken smooth shore only her own foot prints disturbed the sand. She felt like Robinson Crusoe and almost wished she too was the only one here; at least then she would have no problems.

The water was blue and tempting and even though she hadn't come prepared Cathy decided impulsively to go for a swim. There was a tiny cove a little further on where no one would see her.

Soon she was swimming happily, enjoying the feeling of being away from it all. Out here it was peaceful, like being in another world. She turned on her back and floated for a while, looking up at the cloudless blue sky.

Even the birds were different here. Not far away bobbed an all-white bird with long tail streamers and a yellow bill. He appeared to be watching her and she called out but he took not the least bit notice. Several others wheeled overhead and she wished she knew what they were.

For several long minutes she allowed herself to drift, not realising exactly how far she had travelled until she decided to return. She was amazed then to see how distant the shore was, but it didn't worry her as she was a strong swimmer.

Even so, by the time she reached it she was totally exhausted, and it was not until she dragged herself up on to the sand that she saw the blood streaming from her leg.

She had been told that coral reefs surrounded part of the island and could only assume that she had caught herself on them without realising it. The blood flowed freely now and it began to feel sore.

She clambered over the rocks, only to find to her horror that her clothes had disappeared. She looked about her, wondering whether she had mistaken the spot, but no, she was sure this was it. Someone must have taken them! But who? She had seen no one, would never have dared go swimming in the nude if she had.

She was panic-stricken, she couldn't very well go back to the house like this. What was she to do? A sudden shout from behind a nearby rock made her look across suspiciously. Grant's head came into view. He was grinning broadly.

'Give me back my clothes!' cried Cathy heatedly, folding her arms ineffectively across her breasts.

He laughed mischievously and came towards her. He wore only a pair of brief black swimming trunks and she could only assume that he had intended to go swimming himself, until he saw her clothes, and then he had decided to play this trick on her. She did not think it was in the least funny, especially when he eyed her naked body hungrily.

'Where are my clothes?' she demanded again hotly. 'I want them!'

'And I want you,' he suggested insolently, and before she could stop him he had taken her into his arms, and the feel of his skin against hers drove all other thoughts out of her head.

'My Cleopatra has turned into a mermaid,' he whispered thickly, entwining his hands into her hair and pulling back her head so that she was compelled to look at him.

His tawny eyes were deep and searching and there was desire on his face exactly as there had been last night when he had asked her to stay with him. But she knew that that was all it was—desire; there was no love in his heart and in no way was she going to allow herself to be used by him. She had had enough of that with Eric.

She struggled frantically. 'Let me go, Grant, I want to get dressed. I'm cold.'

'I'll keep you warm,' he smiled.

'I don't want you to!' she cried frantically, even though her heart told her otherwise.

'You have a beautiful body,' he said, his hands stroking and caressing, pulling her towards him so that she was virtually aware of his need of her. Contact between them was dynamic.

It was always like this, when he touched her. He sent uncontrollable shivers through her body, feelings more intense than she had ever known existed. If only he loved her too it would have been so perfect. As it was she must never let herself give in to him, that would be the beginning of the end so far as she was concerned.

Her struggles intensified and Grant eventually relaxed his hold, but even so he did not let her go completely. He still held her hands, a couple of feet only between them. His eyes devoured her body slowly and thoroughly so that Cathy felt her awareness deepen.

Suddenly he noticed the blood dripping from her leg and giving an exclamation of surprise he dropped to his knees, examining the wound.

'What the hell have you done?' he demanded. 'Why didn't you tell me?'

'I'd forgotten about it;' she admitted. Grant's presence had seen to that, but now she became immediately aware of the pain shooting up her leg.

'You must get that seen to at once,' he said, and he sounded angry, as though accusing her of negligence, when in fact it was his fault that she had not returned to the house immediately.

Turning swiftly, he fetched her clothes from behind the rock. He tore a strip from the hem of her dress and bandaged the injured leg. She picked up what was left of the dress and shrugged into it.

They were less than halfway home when she began to limp, the pain becoming more intense with each step that she took.

Grant swore and swung her into his arms. 'Of all the damn fool tricks to do! How did you manage it?'

'I don't know,' she confessed. 'I went for a swim and when I got back I found this. I suppose I must have caught it on some coral.'

'Then you went too far out,' he said savagely. 'My God, you're a silly child sometimes. You want to count yourself lucky that this is all you've done. The coral's razor-sharp, didn't you know that?'

'I didn't see it,' Cathy said. She wouldn't admit that she had been looking at the birds instead of where she was going; Grant would have regarded that as sheer stupidity.

He took her directly into the kitchen and sat her on a chair. He did not seem in the least exerted by having had to carry her, he was not even breathing heavily. She marvelled at his physical fitness.

The rag about her leg was bright red. He fetched it

off and cleaned the wound carefully with antiseptic, exclaiming loudly when he saw how deep and long it was.

'It will need stitching,' he said.

'Nonsense,' said Cathy. 'It will soon heal, it's nothing.'

Her awareness of the man kneeling at her side was so intense it made her feel irritable. She wondered how he could have one moment declared he wanted her and the next act with such clinical detachment. Never did her body stop aching for him, proving yet again that his feelings for her in no way compared with her own.

As Grant was applying the bandage Eric came into the kitchen. He was unshaven and his face looked pasty, his eyes bleary. Cathy wondered how she could have ever thought herself in love with him.

He frowned when he saw what Grant was doing. 'What happened?'

Without looking up Grant said, 'She cut her leg on some coral. The silly child went out swimming too far.'

'Swimming—this time in the morning?' yawned Eric. 'You must be mad!'

He had never been much of an athlete, Cathy knew, and she despised him all the more for it now, comparing him unconsciously with Grant. Grant was physical fitness to perfection. His superb body contained not an ounce of superfluous flesh. He was muscular, tanned, healthy, a perfect specimen of manhood.

It had taken him to make her realise what sort of a man Eric was, and when Eric poured himself a cup of coffee from the percolator Grant must have plugged in before coming down to the beach, she loathed him even more. She could have broken her leg for all the interest he was taking.

When he had finished Grant insisted she remain seated while he cooked their breakfast. 'Mrs P.'s not coming in today,' he said, and she guessed why. The housekeeper had made her dislike of Eric all too clear.

It was the first time she had seen Grant working in the kitchen and she was surprised at how adept he was. Quite shortly he placed a plate of bacon and eggs before her. 'I still believe in good old English breakfasts,' he said, smiling, 'especially after an early morning swim in the altogether.'

Eric looked at her sharply and not surprisingly she felt the need to defend herself. 'I didn't plan to go swimming, I only meant to go for a walk, but there was no one about and the sea was so tempting——'

'Except Grant,' cut in Eric viciously.

'Grant wasn't there when I began my swim.'

'But needless to say it wasn't long before he joined you?'

'I was on hand when she needed me,' interrupted Grant smoothly. 'It's fortunate I was. She'd never have made it back with that leg.'

'Am I supposed to believe that's all you did?' snarled Eric. 'I know you too well, Grant, to accept that.'

Grant shrugged laconically. 'Ask Cathy.'

But when Eric looked at her Cathy recalled the feel of Grant's naked body against her own and swift colour flooded her cheeks.

'Don't bother to answer,' said Eric. 'I'll draw my own conclusions.'

'You'd do that anyway,' remarked Grant. 'But as

you've no more interest in Cathy I don't see that it's any concern of yours.'

'It shouldn't be,' he admitted, 'but since I was responsible for her coming here I do have an interest in her well being.'

'How very big of you,' returned Grant. 'A pity you didn't think that way when you sent her.'

'I didn't think she'd——' Eric broke off abruptly and Cathy had the horrible feeling that he had been going to say, 'fall in love with you.'

She was grateful he had stopped in time, but unfortunately he had aroused Grant's interest.

He said now, 'Go on, Eric, I should be interested to hear what you were going to say.'

Eric shook his head looking guilty for once, which surprised Cathy because he was usually adept at covering his feelings. 'Nothing,' he said.

'You mean nothing that Cathy would want me to know?'

'Something like that,' shrugged Eric.

To Cathy's relief Grant let the subject drop and after breakfast he announced that he would be spending the rest of the day in his study. She immediately offered to help, but he insisted she rest her leg.

'For goodness' sake,' she protested, 'it's only a scratch! I'm not an invalid.'

'Even so,' he said, 'it's deep, you need to be careful. Besides, I'm sure Eric will be pleased of your company.'

Eric said quickly, 'I don't think I could stand being cooped up here all day. I'm off to the hotel to mix with the guests.'

Grant smiled and Cathy knew what he was thinking.

He knew exactly what Eric's game was. He had had no intention of buying Samora and keeping it as it was, it was far too sleepy. Eric was a gregarious character.

In a way, thought Cathy, it would be a relief to get rid of him. She would get another of Grant's books and sit out on the terrace.

As soon as breakfast was over Eric went to his room, reappearing a few minutes later freshly shaven and dressed in immaculate white shirt and slacks. He went without saying goodbye.

Grant helped Cathy upstairs, despite her insistence that she could manage alone, and she changed into a clean dress before he settled her comfortably on a lounger on the terrace, a pile of magazines at her side.

But she was not interested in the magazines. She waited until he was in his study and then limped through into the garden room and selected another of his books.

She had lost all sense of time when he later came out to make sure she was all right. He frowned when he saw what she was reading.

'Where did you get that from?'

'I fetched it,' she said.

'You could have asked me.'

'I thought you'd object. I thought you might not like me reading your books.'

'Since you've read most of the others I can't see that it matters,' he said sharply.

There was only one book that he did not want her to read, she thought, and it still intrigued her. It was so different. This one, for instance, was about an ace bomber pilot and held none of the sentiment contained in the pages he was now writing. Had she not known otherwise she would have thought that the author was an entirely different person.

'Would you like coffee or lime juice?' he asked abruptly.

Cathy guessed he did not want to discuss his writing. Maybe he thought she would bring up the subject of his present book. 'Lime, please, but you really needn't bother. I know you want to get on with your work.'

He shrugged. 'It's not going too good this morning. I might have known it was a waste of time with my household disrupted.'

'I'm sorry about Eric,' she said. 'I had no idea he'd turn up.'

'I'm not,' said Grant shortly. 'He had to show some display of concern, just in case you had succeeded in doing what he wanted.'

'You mean becoming friends with you?'

He nodded. 'It's what he wanted, but I don't somehow think he likes it now it's happened.'

'I wouldn't say that we were good friends,' said Cathy distantly.

'Nor are we enemies,' he replied.

'I feel we are sometimes,' she said. 'You couldn't say that ours is the best of relationships.'

He looked at her closely. 'Will you be glad when you've gone?'

It was almost as though he cared, which was ridiculous when she thought about it. Was he truly disappointed that she had not agreed to become his mistress? 'In one way,' she replied, 'although I shall be sorry to leave Samora. I've grown to love it.'

She wanted to ask whether he would be glad when she'd gone, whether the fact that she had turned down his offer to stay had meant anything to him, or whether he had taken it in his stride and couldn't really care less.

He disappeared into the house and came back a few minutes later with the lime. He joined her and she wondered whether he was going to do any more writing that day.

She found it difficult to breathe when he was near. All the while her senses were vitally alive, she wanted to reach out and touch him, she wanted him to crush her in his arms. She wanted so much! No doubt she could have it still, on his terms, but no matter how much she loved him she couldn't do that.

It would appear that he was not free to marry her, why else had he suggested she become his mistress? Or perhaps he was free but he didn't love her, merely found her body physically exciting?

'How's the leg?' he asked presently.

'It's all right while I'm resting,' she said, 'but it hurts when I put any weight on it.'

Grant frowned. 'I'll change the dressing later, one can't be too careful in this climate.'

'I can manage myself,' said Cathy, not realising how terse she sounded.

He frowned. 'You object to me touching you all of a sudden?'

Not object, she said to herself. I love the feel of your hands on my body, but it's not doing me any good. 'I don't want to put you to any trouble,' she lied. 'I've been enough nuisance as it is.'

'You sorted my files,' he said. 'I'm grateful. I was after something last night and found it straight away.' He sounded surprised. 'I shall miss you. You've been very useful.'

'Considering you didn't want me in the first place,' said Cathy drily, 'I suppose that's a compliment.'

'It's not often I hand them out,' he admitted. 'You're an exception. But then you're an exceptional girl.'

Except in the way that mattered most, she thought dispiritedly. She sighed. 'I feel guilty sitting here, are you sure there's nothing I can do?'

He got to his feet and held out his hand. 'You can keep me company while I prepare lunch.'

'Isn't it rather early?' she protested.

'Perhaps, but I thought I'd get it ready and then we can eat when we feel like it. I doubt if Eric will be back. I can't see him returning until late, so we have the whole day in front of us.'

A whole day of enforced inactivity, thought Cathy, and if Grant was going to stay at her side it was going to be unbearable.

She struggled up and allowed him to help her into the kitchen, fighting primitive instincts to press her body close to his. Damn the man, she thought. Why does he have this effect on me?

'I think I'll go to my room later,' she said to his back as he worked at the sink. 'Lie down on my bed for a while.'

She saw him tense. 'Had enough of my company?' he barked in sudden anger, 'and using your leg as an excuse? I'm sorry I suggested it.'

She would never have enough of his company, but how could she tell him that without giving herself away? 'I merely thought you'd get on with your writing without me.'

'I've already told you that I'm not going to do any more today,' he said impatiently. 'If you're frightened of being alone with me I'll fetch my parents.'

'Oh, please do,' said Cathy quickly, trying to ignore his harsh scowl. 'It's been ages since I saw them.' She knew he would misinterpret her reaction, but perhaps it was best this way.

Grant did not speak again and as soon as he had finished getting their meal ready he disappeared. He had been remarkably tetchy since Eric arrived and Cathy could not imagine why. It was not as though he cared for her. He would never have suggested their living together without the trappings of marriage if he did.

But why had he seemed disquieted when she expressed a wish to shut herself away? The more she thought about it the more puzzled she became, and she was glad when he eventually came back with his parents.

Martha was all concern over Cathy's leg and insisted on having a look at it herself. The bleeding had stopped, but as soon as the lint was pulled off it started again. Martha put on a clean dressing, tutting to herself all the time, remarking, as had her son, that it ought really to have a stitch in it.

Grant joined them for lunch and then afterwards he disappeared. Cathy supposed he had gone to try and get on with his book. She hoped he would succeed. She really did feel guilty about stopping him.

Martha and Jonathan chatted volubly and all that Cathy had to do was put in a word here and there, pretend that she was interested in what they were saying, when all the time her thoughts were with Grant.

He had told them that her fiancé had turned up and Martha plied her with questions about Eric, showing concern when she learned that their engagement was over. 'Grant didn't tell me that,' she said, puzzled. 'What happened?'

'A mutual decision,' said Cathy tonelessly, and Martha did not press the issue.

Instead she turned the subject to her son. 'It's about time he finished his book, he's been on it long enough. It seems to be taking more out of him than usual. Has he discussed it with you?'

Cathy shook her head; not for anything would she admit to having stolen a glance at his manuscript. 'He says he never lets anyone read his work before it's published.'

'Nonsense,' scoffed his mother. 'Quite often I've checked through them for him, but if that's what he wants, so be it. I've never even asked him about this one, not since the beginning when I enquired what it was about and he almost snapped my head off. I thought then it was unusual, but I learned long ago never to push my nose in where it's not wanted.'

Later Martha cooked their evening meal and Grant made a pretence of being friendly, although Cathy could tell it was all an act. Was he disturbed because of her? she wondered.

He was a strange man, she was never able to understand his moods from one minute to the next.

When eventually it was time for his parents to go Cathy said that most probably she would be in bed before he got back. 'I'm tired,' she said, 'sitting around all day has made me even more tired than usual.'

But they had gone no more than ten minutes when Eric returned. She thought it was a wonder he hadn't bumped into them, but apparently he hadn't. He had been drinking and greeted her enthusiastically, almost as though their engagement was still on.

'You look as though you've enjoyed your day, Eric,' she said, and attempted to pull out of his arms. 'I'm off to bed now, to rest my leg—goodnight.'

But his grip tightened and she was surprised. Eric had never been like this in the old days. It must be the drink. 'Let me go!' she insisted, but he laughed, an ugly laugh, and held her even tighter.

His kisses repulsed her and she was surprised, because it was no more than a few days ago that she had contemplated marrying him.

'You're not really in love with Grant Howard?' he questioned thickly. 'I'm as wealthy as he is, Cathy. I can give you anything he can.'

It was the drink that was talking and although at one time she might have been flattered had he spoken to her like this she was wiser now. 'You used me, Eric,' she said tightly. 'You admitted that. Do you really think I have any feeling left for you?'

'We'll see,' he grated harshly, and dragged her down on to the settee.

She had never known him like this before. He had never given her more than a perfunctory kiss, and she did not like the mood he was in. 'Leave me alone!' she cried savagely, twisting to free herself.

But he was like an animal, pawing and clawing, and the more she struggled the more determined he became to subjugate her. In the end she lay still, allowing him to kiss her but remaining unresponsive in the hope that he would get fed up when he realised it was getting him nowhere.

When she heard the door open she knew Grant was back and tried to sit up, wanting to assure him that this was none of her doing. But it closed again firmly and it was too late. He had drawn his own conclusions!

There was even less chance now of him ever returning her love.

'Grant's home,' she said insistently to Eric, and whether it was actually because of that or because he realised he was getting nowhere, he got up, and crossing to the cabinet poured himself a drink.

'Don't you think you've had enough?' she asked crossly.

He shrugged. 'One more won't hurt. Go to bed if you like. Go to Grant. Perhaps he'll get more response out of you.'

She felt disgusted watching Eric's bloated, drunken face, and tossing her head she left, limping up to her bedroom, half expecting to find Grant waiting to confront her. But all was quiet and contrary to what she expected Cathy fell immediately asleep.

The next morning she felt apprehensive, wondering what sort of reception she was going to get from the two men. It was not Eric who bothered her, she couldn't care less about him, it was Grant. He thought she had been agreeable to Eric's caresses, and how was she going to convince him otherwise?

To her relief there was no sign of him when she went downstairs. Coffee bubbled in the percolator, but that was all.

Cathy poured herself a cup and sat at the table. Only one more day, she thought. Tomorrow the boat would come and she would be free of them both.

She would also be jobless, she decided sadly, and it was going to be difficult to find another one. But there was no way that she was going to continue working for Eric, even if he wanted her. She knew that if she asked he would probably find her a job somewhere else in the company, but she wanted nothing more to do with Bassett Holdings. She wanted nothing to remind her of him—or Grant.

Long after she had finished her coffee Cathy still sat there. Her leg was not so painful this morning, she could walk quite easily without that stabbing pain. She toyed with the idea of going down to Martha and Jonathan's, but it was a long way and although she felt no discomfort at the moment she knew full well that her leg might not stand up to the walk. It would be wiser to remain here, even though it was the last thing that she wanted.

She did not know whether Grant was in his study or whether he had left the house. She had not heard his typewriter as she passed, but that did not mean he was not there. Should she disturb him? Go and see if there was anything she could do?

But she was afraid—afraid that after what he had seen last night he might berate her, tell her she was an idiot for allowing herself to be swayed by Eric. He would not know that she had protested, that she had struggled against his advances to no avail. He would only believe what he had seen. It was perhaps far better to keep away.

She was still sitting there when Mrs P. arrived and the housekeeper did not look too pleased to find her kitchen occupied.

Cathy rose immediately. 'I'm just going.'

Mrs Prim looked down at Cathy's leg, but said nothing. Cathy had not expected her to. The housekeeper would not concern herself about her, though exactly why she resented her presence was still a mystery.

She went out on to the terrace, sitting down on one of the wrought iron chairs. But she felt restless and did not stay for long, making her way down the steps and into the garden, walking across the smooth green lawns, stopping here and there to sniff one of the exotic flowers.

She thought how nice it would be to live here and learn the names of these excitingly different plants and birds. To share all this with Grant would have made her the happiest woman in the world.

When she returned to the house Eric was sitting on the terrace. He did not look too good. 'How are you feeling?' Cathy asked, not really caring. She hoped he had a king-sized hangover. She hoped his head was splitting—he deserved it!

He mumbled something and she carried on into the house and through into the gardens at the back. They were completely separate here from the front and she had never had the time to explore them.

They were built on several levels and as she climbed each lot of steps she found completely different types of gardens. But it was not until she reached the very top of the hill where the garden led over the summit with a few tall trees pointing their way skywards that she saw Grant.

He was sitting several yards away from her on a bench beneath what looked like a weeping willow. He seemed lost in thought and she was quite sure that he hadn't seen her. She wondered whether to go or retreat quickly.

But as she stood there he looked across. Unable to help herself, Cathy walked slowly towards him and he moved up so that she could sit at his side. His face was unreadable, cold and distant, and she assumed it had something to do with last night.

'I never knew this part of the garden existed,' she

said, trying to sound cheerful. 'It's beautiful, Grant. Do you often sit out here?'

'Only when I have something on my mind,' he said abruptly.

'Like when your book's not going well?' she suggested, deliberately misinterpreting his meaning.

'Sometimes that,' he admitted.

She did not press the matter further, mentally crossing her fingers that he would not bring up the subject of Eric, but she might have known that it was futile. For a few long tense seconds he strummed his fingers on the bench beside him, and then turning his head he exclaimed, 'Damn it, Cathy, why did you have to do that?'

'Do what?' she asked innocently.

'You know,' he snapped. 'Why did you have to let Eric make love to you?'

'He did no such thing,' she denied hotly.

'Are you trying to tell me that I didn't see you lying on the settee with him, that I didn't see you returning his kisses?'

She shrugged. 'I'm not denying that, Grant. After all, he was once my fiancé. My feelings for him are not completely dead.'

'So I've noticed,' he ground savagely.

'I really don't see that it's any concern of yours.' Cathy began to feel annoyed. What did it matter to him what she did? If he had indicated any feelings for her then it would have been different, but he had made it quite clear he considered her an intruder and that he would be relieved when she eventually left the island.

'While you are in my house,' he said tersely, 'I do feel that I have a certain say in what goes on.'

'To the extent of ruling my private affairs?' she asked crossly.

'If I think you're making a fool of yourself, yes,' he replied. 'You know damn well that Eric's been stringing you along, so why let this happen now? If you're feeling frustrated I'm more than willing to oblige.'

'I've no doubt about that,' snapped Cathy. 'You're as bad as Eric! He used me to try and get the island, you're using me purely to satisfy your own lust. I shall be glad when I've gone!'

He frowned savagely. 'It will be a relief to me too,' he said, 'perhaps then I shall be able to get on with my writing.'

CHAPTER EIGHT

CATHY and Grant stared at each other hostilely for several minutes. At length she said with quiet dignity, 'I don't see how you can accuse me of being the cause of your not being able to write. I never interrupt you. I always keep myself very much to myself.'

'You're attractive enough to keep any man from his work,' he ground bitterly.

'Am I supposed to feel flattered?' she asked hotly. 'Anyone would think I went around deliberately flaunting myself!'

'And don't you?' he demanded. 'I seem to remember on that first day that you——'

'Oh, go to hell!' she snapped savagely, pushing herself up and marching back towards the house.

Mrs Prim met her, a tray of drinks in her hand, her face even more dour than usual. 'Where is everyone?' she demanded.

'Here and there,' said Cathy. 'Let them get their own.' She picked up a cup and left Mrs P. grumbling loudly to herself.

By lunchtime there was still no sign of either of the men and Cathy ate a solitary meal. Was Grant still sitting up there on the hill? she mused. Had he lost all sense of time, or was he still so disgusted by her behaviour that he did not want to see her again? Perhaps he was keeping out of her way.

And Eric, where had he gone? Back down to the hotel? Was he going to get drunk yet again?

After lunch she finished reading Grant's book about the bomber pilot, and when she went to put it back on its shelf he was there, standing by the fireplace, a glass of whisky in his hand.

'You haven't eaten,' she said accusingly. 'Do you really think you ought to be drinking?'

'It's no business of yours,' he snapped.

But she had had enough of Eric last night without wanting to see Grant in the same position. 'Can I fetch you a sandwich?' she asked patiently. 'Mrs P. cleared lunch away ages ago.'

'If I was hungry,' he said with quiet menace, 'I'm perfectly capable of getting it for myself. Just leave me alone.'

'You mean you don't want to see me again before I leave?' she asked, and inside she was crying.

'Something like that,' he said coldly.

Cathy turned swiftly and left. He hadn't even asked how her leg was this morning. It really would be a good job when the boat came. The situation here was becoming impossible.

She wondered whether either of the men would put in an appearance at dinner. She knew that if she was Mrs Prim, and had been treated like she had today, she would not bother. She would leave. If anyone wanted anything they could get it for themselves!

It came as no surprise therefore when the housekeeper sought her out later in the afternoon. 'I'm off now,' she said crisply. 'I don't know where Mr Howard or your boy-friend are.'

'That's all right,' said Cathy. 'I'll get their dinner. I understand.'

And for once the forbidding woman allowed herself to smile.

'I'm leaving tomorrow,' Cathy told her. 'I don't know what time, but in case I don't see you again I'll say goodbye now. I apologise if I've been a nuisance.'

Mrs P.'s eyes softened slightly. 'That's all right,' she said, and then she had gone.

It was as well that she hadn't bothered to cook, thought Cathy later, when neither of the men put in an appearance. She was not feeling particularly hungry herself, but she ate a cold chicken sandwich and then, although it was only half past eight, she went to her room and undressed ready for bed.

She lay there a long time, unconsciously listening for sounds of Grant. But the house was eerily quiet and she knew she had it to herself. She toyed with the idea of going down and reading some more of his new book, but was afraid he might come back and catch her.

When she heard heavy footsteps on the stairs Cathy was on the verge of falling asleep. They stopped occasionally and then a dull sound like someone lurching against the wall. It was Eric, she thought disgustedly, drunk again!

She heard him go into his room and a thud as he fell on to the bed, then all was quiet. He was in a drunken stupor, she decided. She supposed really she ought to go in to him, make sure he was all right, but she couldn't bring herself to do it. He revolted her. She had never seen him like this before, but then again she was seeing him on this island in a new light.

She wondered why it had never occurred to her in the beginning that this was not the sort of place Eric would enjoy. He always liked to be in a crowd. It was very rare they had gone anywhere alone. She ought to have known this sleepy little island was not his scene.

He was getting drunk now because he was bored, because there was nothing to do. Cathy could only feel relief that he had not managed to persuade Grant to sell. In no time at all he would have desecrated Samora, he would have turned it into a tourist's paradise with dance halls and casinos, tennis courts and bowling alleys.

About an hour later Grant too returned, but he came up the stairs so quietly that she had to strain her ears. His door closed with a little click and then all was silent again in the big house.

Cathy could not sleep, though. She was too keyed up by the events of the day, too disturbed by Grant's treatment of her to allow herself to relax sufficiently to sleep. She managed to doze off and on, tossing and turning throughout the whole night.

She heard Grant go downstairs but nothing from Eric's room. She presumed he was still sleeping off the effects of the drink. Distasteful though she found the task she knew she would have to go in and wake him. She had no idea what time the boat was coming, but she did not want to miss it.

Eric was still lying across the bed, fully clothed, and she felt sickened. She shook his shoulder and he groaned. She shook him harder and at length he opened his eyes. They were bleary and she doubted he could see her clearly.

'Eric,' she said firmly, 'you must get up. What time's the boat coming?'

He looked at her blankly. 'Ten o'clock, I think,' and he frowned.

'In that case,' she said urgently, 'you'd better hurry. It's already nearly nine, I should hate to miss it.'

He sat up and groaned, putting a hand to his head.
'I'll fetch you some tablets,' she said harshly. 'Get yourself washed and cleaned up.'

But when she got back he still sat exactly where she had left him. His eyes were closed and his face ghastly.

'Eric,' she said loudly, 'come on, you must get ready.' She pushed the glass of water into his hand and held out the tablets.

He groped awkwardly, but managed to pick them up and push them into his mouth. He swallowed down the glass of water eagerly and seemed a little better after that, but Cathy refused to go out of the room until she was sure he was going to get himself ready.

She went down into the kitchen. Coffee was already percolating. She poured him a cup in readiness and was drinking her own when Grant appeared.

'What time are you going?' he asked abruptly.

You needn't sound so eager, she thought; you needn't look so eager. 'The boat's coming at ten.'

'Then you'll have to look sharp. What's keeping Eric?'

'He's drunk again,' she said bitterly.

'Again?' and he frowned. 'Was he drunk the night before, when he made that pass at you?'

She nodded.

'Why didn't you tell me?'

'I thought you realised.'

'I thought you were enjoying it. If I'd known I'd have slung him out.'

'It's only because he's bored,' said Cathy, trying to defend him.

'As well he might be in this place,' growled Grant. 'It's not his scene.'

'Which I'm beginning to realise,' she returned sadly.

He looked at her sharply. 'I'll go and see if he needs any help.'

Soon the two of them were back down. Eric had on a fresh shirt and trousers and Grant held his case. He also carried Cathy's which she had left on her bed already packed.

He certainly was eager to see them go, she thought dispiritedly. Eric drank the black coffee and she poured him another cup, and then they left. Grant came with them down the hill. He must want to make sure they really went, she thought.

When they reached the small jetty the boat was waiting. Cathy was relieved. She had no wish to stand around with the two men. Conversation would have been impossible and they would all three have felt uncomfortable.

She held out her hand to Grant. 'Goodbye, Mr Howard. Thank you for putting me up. I hope I didn't hold up your writing too much.'

He inclined his head coolly. 'Goodbye, Cathy.'

And that was all!

A few minutes later they were speeding towards the Seychelles. Cathy could not resist turning back, but Grant had already disappeared. Tears sprang to her eyes and she dashed them away angrily. What use was there in getting upset? It had been a one-sided affair all along.

When they reached Mahé she discovered that their flight was only a matter of half an hour's wait. Things were moving swiftly now.

She and Eric scarcely spoke on the journey home and when they arrived in London he bundled her into a taxi and she realised that most probably this was the last time she would ever see him.

Cathy had always enjoyed living in London, but now she could not stand the place. In contrast to Samora's green freshness and flaming tropical colours London seemed grey and dismal, and although it teemed with people it was a far less friendly place.

She had been back a week when the letter came, a week during which she had cried herself to sleep every night. She realised that she would never see Grant again, but this did not stop her thinking about him. Her love instead of fading seemed to grow stronger with every passing day and the ache in her heart deepened.

The letter was from her aunt who lived on the outskirts of the market town of Shrewsbury. She invited Cathy to spend a long holiday with them.

Cathy wrote back at once accepting; it was just the tonic she needed. On an impulse she gave up her flat, deciding that she would find somewhere nearer her aunt to live, or at least somewhere well away from London.

Her Aunt Kathleen, her mother's sister, welcomed her warmly, effusively, but frowned when she saw the girl's drawn face and shadowed eyes. 'My dear child, you look positively ill! It seems like my invitation came just in time. Fresh air, plenty of sleep and lots of good wholesome food, that's what you need.'

Cathy smiled wanly. It suited her to let her aunt think that her paleness was due to living and working in London. 'As a matter of fact,' she said to her aunt, 'I've given up my flat. I think I might find myself somewhere round here to live. I've decided I've had enough living in the city.'

Her aunt was delighted. 'You can make your home with us,' she said decisively. 'It's what your dear mother would have wanted. I never did hold with you going off down there by yourself. But what about your fiancé, Eric what's-his-name? What's he got to say about you leaving?'

'The engagement's over,' said Cathy.

And her aunt wisely did not pursue the matter, probably thinking that this was the reason for Cathy's jaded looks.

Her uncle was out at work, but when he came home that evening he too professed concern over Cathy's appearance. 'Plenty of fresh air in your lungs, that's what you want,' he said, unconsciously reiterating his wife's words.

During the weeks that followed Cathy's memories of her few days on Samora faded, although she knew that she would never wipe Grant completely from her heart.

Roses bloomed again in her cheeks and her eyes resumed their customary sparkle. When at length she protested that she had put on her aunt and uncle for long enough and that she was going to find a job and somewhere else to live, they were indignant.

'This is your home for as long as you like,' said her aunt, 'although I do think you could be right about a job. I'll make some enquiries. That big bookshop in town was after an assistant the other day, I'll see if they still want one.'

It was not often that they watched television. Her aunt and uncle were always out in the garden until it got dark, and then after supper it was time for bed.

Cathy would either help or go for long walks along the country lanes. She found it best to tire herself out, then she fell asleep almost immediately.

But one night when rain forced them to come in from the garden early her uncle switched on the television. A chat show was in progress, and Cathy's eyes nearly fell out when she saw Grant.

She sat forward in her seat, her eyes riveted to the set, taking in every word that Grant said. The interviewer asked whether he was working on a book at the moment, and to Cathy's total surprise he said no. He said he was taking a well earned rest and that he had no plans yet for another novel.

It must mean, she thought, that he had finished it, but wanted no one to know at this stage about the different type of work that he had attempted. She could understand his feelings, having read the novel herself, because there was no comparison to the style of writing that had earned him his reputation.

He looked exactly the same as she remembered. He wore an open-necked shirt and his hair was awry as usual. Cathy had not realised that her aunt and uncle were aware of her interest, not until the programme finished and her Aunt Kathleen asked, 'Why were you so intent in what Howard Grant was saying? Are you a fan of his?'

Cathy smiled wryly. 'I've read some of his books. They're very good.'

'You seemed to take more than a normal interest,' said her uncle. 'Fancy him, do you?' and there was a twinkle in his eye. 'I'm afraid the likes of him are a little out of your reach.'

Cathy nodded. 'I don't suppose he'd even notice me if I was in the same room.'

'Now, now,' reproved the older woman. 'You're a very pretty girl, you'd turn any man's head.'

But not Grant Howard's, thought Cathy sadly, and she was about to change the conversation when her aunt said:

'There was something about him in the paper the other day. I'm trying to think what it was—oh, I know, he's doing a tour of the major towns promoting his latest book.'

Cathy hardly thought that likely, it couldn't possibly be ready for publication yet. But he had told her, now she came to think about it, that he had a book due for publication some time this year, one about sunken treasure.

He had told her that he enjoyed the research immensely, that he had never realised what a different world there was on the sea bed. 'If I hadn't been a writer,' he had said, 'I think I would have liked to be a deep sea diver.'

She wondered whether Shrewsbury was included in his promotion tour, and would have dearly liked to ask her aunt, but was afraid that if she showed too much interest they might question her further.

Fortunately her aunt volunteered the information. 'I do believe he's coming to Shrewsbury,' she said. 'I'll find out. You'll be able to get an autographed copy.'

'That will be nice,' said her uncle, 'especially you being a fan of his.'

The next day Cathy's aunt told her that Howard Grant would be at the big bookshop in Shrewsbury in four weeks' time. 'You know, the one where the job was going. I went in today to see about it for you and they were all talking about his visit. The job's been filled, unfortunately, or you might have been able to talk to him. But never mind, we'll still go. I've never met a celebrity before, it should be fun.'

Fun wasn't exactly the word Cathy would have used, and although she allowed her aunt to make plans she had no intention of speaking to Grant, she would keep well out of his way.

During the weeks that followed Cathy could not get out of her mind the thought that soon Grant would be here, that he would be only a matter of a few miles away, and that if she so wished she could go and speak to him again.

Her heart fluttered each time she thought of him, her love flooding to the surface. She dreamt of him at night, far-fetched dreams in which he asked her to marry him, declaring that he had searched the whole of England for her.

She would wake from these dreams feeling euphoria, only to find it fading when the stark reality of day was upon her and she realised that nothing like this would ever happen.

The day before his visit Cathy caught a cold. Her nose and eyes streamed and it hurt to swallow. When she showed no sign of improvement the next morning her aunt stated firmly that she must spend the day in bed.

'I'll go into Shrewsbury and get a book for you,' she said. 'I know how much you were looking forward to it.'

Cathy did not protest. It was as though this had to be. She had always known that there was no use in her trying to see Grant again. She meant nothing to him, if she had he would not have let her go so easily, or at least he would have tried to find her.

So many weeks had passed since she left Samora

that if he had really been interested she was quite sure he could have found out where she had gone.

The house was empty, her aunt had left and her uncle was at work. Cathy lay in bed staring at the faint cracks in the ceiling. She felt miserable and sorry for herself. She could hardly see out of her eyes and her whole body ached. She spent her time between bouts of shivering and intense warmth.

Her aunt had left her some tablets and a glass of fresh orange juice, insisting that she have plenty to drink. 'I shall be back in time for lunch,' she said, 'so don't try to get up.'

Cathy hadn't the strength, even if she'd wanted to. It was all she could do to limp her way to the bathroom and back. Even the thought that she was missing catching a glimpse of Grant did not bother her any more, she felt so ill.

When her aunt returned she took one look at Cathy and phoned for the doctor. It was a couple of hours before he came. ' 'Flu,' he announced after examining her. 'There's an epidemic about. You'll have to stay in bed for a few days and it will be a couple of weeks at least before you're feeling your normal self.'

It was not until after the doctor had left that her aunt remembered the book. 'My goodness!' she exclaimed. 'It had completely slipped my mind, worrying about you.' She fetched it from her bag and handed it to her niece.

Watery Hell, it was called, and Cathy smiled to herself. Hell was one of Grant's favourite words. She opened the book eager to read the inscription. She knew what his handwriting was like, bold flowing lines, and always with a black pen. She had seen it often enough to tell it anywhere.

'To Cathy,' she read, 'In appreciation, Grant Howard.'

She raised startled eyes to her aunt, wondering what interpretation she had put on this.

'Why didn't you tell us you knew him, Cathy? You can imagine my surprise when he asked me whose name I wanted in the book and I told him yours—and he said he knew you. You've kept that a secret.'

'We have met,' admitted Cathy.

'But why the appreciation?' asked her aunt. 'What's that all about?'

'I did some filing for him once. He—he needed—his secretary had left him in the lurch.' She tried to make light of it so that her aunt wouldn't probe further.

But the older woman's curiosity was aroused. 'When was this? You never told us in your letters.'

'Not long before I came here,' admitted Cathy. 'He lives on an island in the Indian Ocean. I'd gone out there for a holiday.'

'A holiday?' Her aunt's puzzlement deepened. 'How could you afford that? Doesn't it cost a fortune going to that sort of place?'

'It was Eric's idea,' said Cathy. 'He wanted to buy me the island for a wedding present.'

Her aunt's eyes widened dramatically. 'A wedding present? Are you sure you did the right thing in finishing with him? He sounds just the right sort of man to marry, plenty of money, you'd never have anything to worry about.'

'I didn't love him. I thought I did, then I found out that I didn't.'

'Then you did the right thing,' said her aunt firmly. 'But I'm wondering whether *I* have. I'm wondering whether I ought to have——' She stopped and looked at Cathy worriedly.

'Ought to have what?'

'Invited Howard Grant here! When he said he knew you it seemed the right thing to do, now I'm not so sure. But don't worry yourself, I've brought you a nice piece of fish for your lunch, I'll go and see to it while you rest. I must have tired you out with all my chatter.'

'When's he coming?' called Cathy as her aunt reached the door.

'I don't know. I told him you were ill, he said he'd phone.'

He wouldn't, thought Cathy tiredly. He had only said that to be polite. Had he wanted to find her he could have easily. She had told her friend in the flat below where she was going, had even left her forwarding address in case any mail arrived.

She had done this because she had half hoped that Grant might get in touch, but as the weeks passed she realised the stupidity of even hoping that he might, and now, even though he knew where she was living, she doubted very much whether he would contact her.

In fact she was not sure that she wanted him to. These last few weeks had taken a lot out of her, she did not feel up to reopening old wounds—because that was what it would be, if they met again. Her love would come bubbling to the surface and she would be left as miserable and unhappy as before.

The fish choked her and she pushed her plate to one side almost untouched. She was relieved that her aunt put it down to the fact that she was ill, did not realise that it had any connection with her conversation with Grant Howard that morning.

Two weeks went by during which time Cathy got slowly better. But of Grant Howard there was no sign, as she had known. Her aunt mentioned him frequently during the first few days, but as time elapsed she referred to him less and less until finally they never spoke about him at all.

Cathy was glad. This was what she needed. She wanted no memories aroused. And then one day when both her aunt and uncle were out the phone rang. It never entered her head that it might be Grant and she answered it cheerfully.

'Cathy?' queried a well remembered voice.

She almost dropped the phone. Her heart beat a familiar tattoo and emotions spiralled up from the pit of her stomach.

'Yes?' she queried cautiously. 'Who's that?' She had to give herself time to think, time to gather her thoughts, decide what she would say to him.

'It's Grant,' he said. 'Remember me?'

As if she would ever forget! 'Oh, hello, Grant. I've read your book, it's very good.'

'I was pleased to meet your aunt,' he said, 'she's a nice woman, it's a pity you were too ill to come along. I should have liked to see you again!'

How banal his words sounded, she thought bitterly, dutiful, as though he had rehearsed every word he meant to say.

When she made no response he continued, 'Your aunt issued an invitation, do you know?'

'Yes,' replied Cathy. 'She told me, but I'm afraid she's out. I'll tell——'

'It's not her I want to see,' he cut in quickly. 'It's you, Cathy. Mind if I come round?'

She shook her head. Oh no, she wanted to cry,

please don't, I couldn't stand it. 'It's not my house,' she said at length. 'You'll have to ring again when my aunt's in.'

'Little liar,' he whispered harshly. 'You don't want to see me, is that it?'

She could imagine his frown, the darkening of those tawny eyes. If only he knew the truth! 'It's not that,' she said hesitantly, 'but——'

'But what?'

Oh, God, she thought, why was he doing this? Why was he tormenting her? He knew exactly the reaction he was able to arouse, so why was he insisting that he come to see her now? 'It's awkward,' she said, 'living in someone else's house. I don't feel free to receive visitors.'

'Since your aunt issued the invitation your argument is invalid,' he said strongly. 'I'll be there in ten minutes.'

'Grant!' she called wildly. 'Grant, wait, you can't——' But the phone had gone dead.

She looked at herself in the mirror. Gosh, what a sight! Quickly she dragged a comb through her hair. It could do with washing, but there wasn't time. She dabbed powder on to her nose—a dash of lipstick. Was there time to change? She decided not, wondering what Grant would think when he saw her in her old jeans and a faded blouse. Since being ill she hadn't bothered with her appearance. She still felt weak and it did not help matters to think about Grant coming now.

She sank down into a chair and closed her eyes, hoping that perhaps it had all been a dream and that in a moment she might wake and find that he was not coming after all.

When the doorbell rang in less than the ten minutes he had given himself she shot up from the chair. She toyed with the idea of ignoring him, pretending that she had gone out. But she knew he was quite capable of breaking down the door, so slowly she made her way into the hall.

She opened the door and stared into the well remembered face. Her heart pounded violently and she stood back for him to enter. 'Please come in,' she said faintly.

He stepped past her, then waited while she closed the door. He was taller than she remembered, more good-looking too, and she could only manage a very weak smile as she led the way into the sitting room.

He wore a suit and a shirt and tie and he looked both familiar and a stranger at the same time. 'My aunt should be home soon,' she said, in an attempt to make conversation, realising how difficult it was going to be to get through the next few minutes. 'She'll be pleased to see you.'

Thick brows frowned strongly. 'It's not your aunt I've come to see.'

'Well, I can't think why you should want to see me,' she protested softly.

'You can't?' He studied her appraisingly. 'Dear Cleopatra, you're exactly as I remember, a little paler, perhaps, but I expect that's because of your illness. I hope it wasn't anything serious?'

' 'Flu,' she answered abruptly. She didn't know why, but she felt uncomfortable in his presence. 'Would you like a cup of tea?'

'I thought you'd never ask,' he mocked, and followed her into the kitchen.

This was the last thing she had wanted, but apart

from telling him there was nothing she could do about it. He perched himself on a stool and watched her movements closely as she assembled cups and saucers.

'Why did you leave London?' he asked suddenly.

'I wanted to get away from Eric,' she lied. It was the first valid excuse that came into her head.

'I've had the devil of a job trying to find you,' he continued. 'If it hadn't been for seeing your aunt the other day I'd still be searching.'

Cathy's mouth fell open, her beautiful blue eyes widened. 'Why did you want to find me?'

'Don't you know?' he asked suggestively.

She shook her head, her black hair swinging. 'I've no idea.'

'Perhaps this will help.' He rose and came towards her, a sensual gleam in his eyes.

Although she wanted to back away it was as though she was hypnotised. His eyes held her own and her breathing felt constricted. Her hand flew up to her throat and then his hands were sliding behind her back, pulling her inexorably against the lean hard strength of him.

She felt as though she was going to faint, her chin lifted automatically, her lips ready to receive his. He kissed her hungrily and her response was equal, the blood pounding in her ears as she clung to Grant, afraid to let him go in case he disappeared out of her life again.

'Oh, God, Cathy,' he groaned. 'I've missed you so much.'

'I've missed you too,' she whispered faintly.

'Promise you'll come back to Samora? I can't live without you, I can't work, I can't do anything.'

She wanted to say yes, but the more logical side of

her nature knew that she would never be happy as Grant's mistress. In the beginning maybe, but after that, when her conscience began prodding her, what then?

'I can't,' she said at length. 'I'm sorry, Grant, but——'

He dashed her away angrily, letting her go so that she fell limply back against the sink. 'Damn it all, Cathy, how can you do this to a man? I've chased you halfway across the world. Doesn't it mean anything to you?'

'You're here on a promotion tour,' she said defensively.

'That too,' he admitted, 'but it's not the only reason. I've scoured the whole of London for you, do you know that?'

'I'm sorry, but I still can't come back to Samora.'

'Is there someone else?' he demanded savagely.

She shook her head.

'Then why the hell not?'

Because I love you too much, she wanted to say. How could she possibly go back with him? The only way would be as his wife. How could she tell him that? Not one word of love had escaped his lips. It was a lover he wanted, but he did not love her, and all Cathy's instincts told her that this was wrong.

When she heard her aunt letting herself into the house she had never been so thankful in all her life. The woman came straight into the kitchen, beaming at Grant. 'I saw a strange car outside, I thought it might be you. I'm glad you've come.'

He shook her hand, smiling warmly. 'You're just in time for tea.'

Once it was made and they had taken their cups into the sitting room she said to Grant, 'Would you like to stop for dinner? Cathy's uncle will soon be home, I know he'll be pleased to meet you. He was so surprised when he found out that Cathy had met you, she never told us.'

'I wonder why that was?' He looked directly at Cathy.

'Cathy's always been reticent,' said her aunt. 'I don't suppose we'd have found out about you at all if she hadn't seen you on the television and shown such an interest.'

He looked amused and Cathy felt like telling her aunt to shut up.

The older woman continued, 'I've read your book, Grant. It was very interesting.'

'You don't have to say that,' he said kindly.

'But I mean it, I thoroughly enjoyed it, Cathy's uncle too. He was more concerned with the fact that you do all your own research. What was it like going down to the ocean bed?'

Cathy sat quietly while they chatted about his latest book and she hoped that he would forget her aunt's invitation to stay to dinner. Perhaps he had a prior engagement? She sincerely hoped so, she did not think she could stand much more of his presence without giving away her feelings.

But her aunt certainly had no intention of letting him escape, and shortly before her husband was due to arrive she excused herself to go into the kitchen and prepare their meal.

Left alone with Grant, Cathy sat uncomfortably staring down at her fingernails. It shouldn't be like this, she thought. If Grant loved her too there would be no unease, they would feel as right together as it is possible for two people to be.

'Something worrying you?' he queried at length, when the silence between them had lengthened into minutes.

When she looked up at him he was relaxed, amused even, smiling as though he knew exactly what was on her mind. 'Why should there be?' she asked defensively. 'Why should there be anything the matter?'

'No reason,' he said, 'but you used not to be like this. You were different when we were on Samora.'

'I was working for you then.'

'And that makes a difference?'

'I wasn't expecting you,' she ventured, realising it was a lame excuse.

'I don't see why that makes it difficult for you to talk to me. Why won't you come to Samora, Cathy?'

His abrupt question took her by surprise and before she could stop herself she said, 'Because I refuse to live with any man as his mistress.'

That did wipe the smile from his face, and he looked at her in complete amazement. 'Is that what you're thinking?'

And when she nodded he groaned and crossing the room pulled her roughly into his arms. 'My dearest, darling Cathy, didn't I make myself clear? It's a wife I want. I love you, Cathy, I want you to marry me. I want you with me for always. Life's been hell since you went away. Please say yes!'

Tears welled in her eyes as he spoke. She could hardly believe what she was hearing.

'B-but your wife,' she managed. 'What about her?'

'My wife's dead,' he said quietly. 'I thought you knew. Didn't my mother tell you?'

Cathy was horrified. 'I had no idea—I'm sorry.'

'Don't be,' he said, holding her even tighter. 'It all happened several years ago. In one way I was thankful, the only thing that upset me was the death of my son.'

Cathy was aghast. 'Both of them?'

He nodded. 'A road accident.'

'You must have been agonised!'

'My wife was a bitch,' he said with sudden savagery. 'She kept Mark away from me, never let me see him. I grew to hate her.'

It suddenly dawned on Cathy that the book he had been writing was his own story, and her heart went out to him. Her tears spilled over, wetting his shirt as she buried her face in his chest. 'Grant,' she muttered, 'I'm so sorry.'

'There's no need,' he said. 'She was like you, Cathy. She had the same dark hair, the same blue eyes.'

'Is that why you resented me when you first saw me, why you pushed me into that horrible little room?'

He nodded. 'I thought you'd turn out like her. I wanted to love you, but I was afraid. It was only after you'd gone that I realised you were in no way like Bernice.'

'I wish you'd told me,' she said. 'It would have made all the difference. I was quite convinced that you still had a wife somewhere and only wanted me as your mistress. I do love you, Grant, I've loved you almost since the first day we met.'

'I know,' he said surprisingly. 'Eric told me. I looked him up in London and he gave me your address. When I found out you'd left I was almost out of my mind, especially knowing that you loved me.'

Cathy frowned. 'But I told my flatmate below where I'd gone—in the vain hope that you might try to find me. I didn't want to disappear without trace, just in case.'

'There was a new girl living there,' he said. 'I tried all the flats, no one knew what had happened to you. I was frantic. You were the only reason I agreed to do this promotion tour. I made a point of mentioning it when I was on television in the hope that you'd hear and somehow try to get in touch with me.'

'We only saw the last part,' admitted Cathy, 'we don't watch much telly, but Aunt Kathleen saw it in the paper, and then she heard the girls talking in the bookshop.'

'I was hoping that you wouldn't be able to stop yourself coming,' he continued. 'I searched the crowds at every bookshop. Oh, my darling Cathy, you don't know what you've done to me! If you don't promise to marry me now I don't think I could bear to go on living.'

'I'll marry you, Grant,' she cried joyfully, 'but I have a confession to make first.'

'Nothing you say will make the slightest difference,' he said confidently, holding her closer so that she felt safe and secure, the most wanted woman in the world.

'I read your book, the one you were writing about yourself, only I didn't realise at the time that it was you, I just knew that it was a strange book for you to write.'

She expected anger, but he smiled. 'I don't mind, but it's not a book for publication. It was just something I had to get out of my system. Now I shan't even bother to finish it. You've done this to me, Cathy.

With you at my side I shall be able to forget the past completely.'

'I promise I'll make you happy,' she said. 'I really will.'

'I've no doubt about that,' he said softly.

His lips possessed hers and for a while time stood still.

Neither heard Cathy's aunt open the door and look into the room, closing it again quietly when she saw the two of them locked into each other's arms, a satisfied smile lightening her kindly face.

The Mills & Boon Rose is the Rose of Romance

COLLISION *by Margaret Pargeter*
After the heartless way Max Heger had treated her, Selena wanted to be revenged on him. But things didn't work out as she had planned.

DARK REMEMBRANCE *by Daphne Clair*
Could Raina marry Logan Thorne a year after her husband Perry's death, when she knew that Perry would always come first with her?

AN APPLE FROM EVE *by Betty Neels*
Doctor Tane van Diederijk and his fiancée were always cropping up in Euphemia's life. If only she could see the back of both of them?

COPPER LAKE *by Kay Thorpe*
Everything was conspiring to get Toni engaged to Sean. But she was in love with his brother Rafe — who had the worst possible opinion of her!

INVISIBLE WIFE *by Jane Arbor*
Vicente Massimo blamed Tania for his brother's death. So how was it that Tania soon found herself blackmailed into marrying him?

BACHELOR'S WIFE *by Jessica Steele*
Penny's marriage to Nash Devereux had been a 'paper' one. So why did Nash want a reconciliation just when Penny wanted to marry Trevor?

CASTLE IN SPAIN *by Margaret Rome*
Did Birdie love the lordly Vulcan, Conde de la Conquista de Retz — who wanted to marry her — or did she fear him?

KING OF CULLA *by Sally Wentworth*
After the death of her sister, Marnie wanted to be left alone. But the forceful Ewan McNeill didn't seem to get the message!

ALWAYS THE BOSS *by Victoria Gordon*
The formidable Conan Garth was wrong in every opinion he held of Dinah — but could she ever make him see it?

CONFIRMED BACHELOR *by Roberta Leigh*
Bradley Dexter was everything Robyn disliked. But now that she could give him a well-deserved lesson, fate was playing tricks on her!

If you have difficulty in obtaining any of these books from your local paperback retailer, write to:

Mills & Boon Reader Service
P.O. Box 236, Thornton Road, Croydon, Surrey, CR9 3RU.
Available August 1981

The Mills & Boon Rose is the Rose of Romance

Every month there are ten new titles to choose from — ten new stories about people falling in love, people you want to read about, people in exciting, far-away places. Choose Mills & Boon. It's your way of relaxing:

July's titles are:

SUMMER FIRE by *Sally Wentworth*
Why had Pandora ensured that the haughty but charming Sir James Arbory would never look at her twice?

CASTLES OF SAND by *Anne Mather*
Little Hussein was Ashley's son, but she must never let him know who she was. How could she put up with the hostility of Hussein's formidable uncle Alain ...

SPITFIRE by *Lindsay Armstrong*
Rod Simpson had bought Bobbie's home and let her stay there. But what happened when his sister got married and went away?

STRANGERS INTO LOVERS by *Lilian Peake*
There was nothing between Gillian Taylor and Randall West any more, except two people, one who loved Gillian and another who loved Randall. And of course, Gary ...

ABDUCTION by *Charlotte Lamb*
The worst thing that had happened to Marisa was for her baby to be snatched. It also brought her estranged husband Gabriel back on the scene ...

ONE OF THE BOYS by *Janet Dailey*
Petra Wallis fell in love with her boss, the dominating Dane Kingston. But he had no more use for her as a woman than as a technician ...

THE FLAME OF DESIRE by *Carole Mortimer*
Sophie's marriage to Luke Vittorio was a mockery. She had the best of reasons for knowing he was still having an affair with her stepmother ...

THE SAVAGE TOUCH by *Helen Bianchin*
Lee was very much attracted to Marc Leone. But nothing was going to deflect her from her real goal in life: to marry a millionaire!

MIXED FEELINGS by *Kerry Allyne*
Kylie's boss, Grant Brandon, was old enough to be her father. So there was no need for his disagreeable nephew, Race Brandon, to be so scathing about her!

A TASTE OF PARADISE by *Margaret Mayo*
Her fiancé had not told Cathy about the unyielding Grant Howard, who lived on the island she had received as a wedding present ...

If you have difficulty in obtaining any of these books from your local paperback retailer, write to:

Mills & Boon Reader Service
P.O. Box 236, Thornton Road, Croydon, Surrey, CR9 3RU.

SAVE TIME, TROUBLE & MONEY!
By joining the exciting NEW...

Mills & Boon Romance CLUB

WITH all these EXCLUSIVE BENEFITS for every member

NOTHING TO PAY! MEMBERSHIP IS FREE TO REGULAR READERS!

IMAGINE the *pleasure* and *security* of having ALL your favourite *Mills & Boon* romantic fiction delivered right to *your* home, absolutely POST FREE... straight off the press! No waiting! No more disappointments! All this PLUS all the latest news of *new books* and *top-selling authors* in your own monthly MAGAZINE... PLUS *regular* big CASH SAVINGS... PLUS lots of wonderful strictly-limited, *members-only* SPECIAL OFFERS! All these exclusive benefits can be *yours* – right NOW – simply by joining the exciting NEW *Mills & Boon* ROMANCE CLUB. Complete and post the coupon below for FREE full-colour leaflet. It costs nothing. HURRY!

No obligation to join unless you wish!

FREE CLUB MAGAZINE Packed with advance news of latest titles and authors

Exciting offers of FREE BOOKS For club members ONLY

Lots of fabulous BARGAIN OFFERS – many at **BIG CASH SAVINGS**

FREE FULL-COLOUR LEAFLET!
CUT OUT CUT OUT COUPON BELOW AND POST IT TODAY!

To: MILLS & BOON READER SERVICE, P.O. Box No 236, Thornton Road, Croydon, Surrey CR9 3RU, England. WITHOUT OBLIGATION to join, please send me FREE details of the exciting NEW Mills & Boon ROMANCE CLUB and of all the exclusive benefits of membership.

Please write in BLOCK LETTERS below

NAME (Mrs/Miss) ....

ADDRESS ....

CITY/TOWN ....

COUNTY/COUNTRY .... POST/ZIP CODE ....

Readers in South Africa and Zimbabwe please write to: P.O. BOX 1872, Johannesburg, 2000. S. Africa